Monica's Journey

By Ferwa Muhammad

Copyright © 2024 Ferwa Muhammad

All rights reserved. This book or parts thereof may not be reproduced in any form, stored in any retrieval system, or transmitted in any form by any means—electronic, mechanical, photocopy, recording, or otherwise—without prior written permission of the publisher, except as provided by United States of America copyright law.

Any references to historical events, real people, or real places are used fictitiously. Names, characters, and places are products of the author's imagination.

ISBN Paperback: 979-88-7667-148-6

To Mrs. Levis and Mrs. Avakian

Mrs. Levis, you may not even remember me, but you'll always be in my heart. Thank you for tutoring me for all those years. I miss you a lot!

Mrs. Avakian, thank you for teaching me so much about writing and helping me branch out of my comfort zone. You are a total inspiration!

Cool Students :)

Riyah McKimmy
Meghana Yathin
Amaya Fasihi
Nicki Atash Sobh
Atusa Aryavand :)
Anjum Masri (writing an amazing book called "The Curse of Vicanham").
Israa (Izzy) Younes
Harshika Rangareddy
Mihir Jain
Alicia Mallon
Abigail (Abby) Domenica
Ella Kassem
Nouria Hamady
Charlotte Sukhenko
Emma Stoltzfus
Emma Nehring
Jad Benjelloun Touimy
Mariam Aziz
Scarlett Stolfa

Table of Contents

Part One 8

Chapter One 10

Chapter Two 30

Chapter Three 53

Chapter Four 72

Flashback 84

Chapter Five 89

Chapter Six 102

Part Two 114

Chapter Seven 115

Chapter Eight 133

Chapter Nine 149

Chapter Ten 164

Chapter Eleven 177

Chapter Twelve 187

About Me! 202

Part One

Her Secrets

✧ Chapter One ✧

Torture is the only word to describe it. The land is full of fear, anxiety, and terror. It is a place in the world that doesn't accept your sentiment. School, your best friend, or your vile enemy. It has a sickening lunch room, revolting cafeteria food, thousands of unique students, and your favorite, the bullies. I am not popular or quiet. I was born straight in the lower tier, where I hope I will always be. I have seven ranks for students. The popular girls, creeps, nerds, jocks, teacher's pets, class clowns, and the bullies. The ranks help determine who's where. I fit in as a nerd, as Mom always told me that doing well in high school would help me get into a good college. I'm one of the luckier nerds, mostly being forgotten in class. Everyone rolls their eyes, hearing our voices. At least I don't have to worry about being the center of attention!

Then again, people would rather kill themselves than have an engaging conversation with me.

Vanessa Blackmore is the most charming person I've ever seen. She has such a solipsistic personality. If jealousy would take a form, it would have her face. She looks like a model with black hair and luscious green eyes. She constantly flexes those traits in front of everyone. All the girls wish they could have a face like her. Kids in school always talk about her being a gossip queen and all. Her malicious actions aren't discussed as she keeps them secret.

You either love school or you hate it, infrequently in the middle. The scale can show your opinions about specific students. School has free drama, but sometimes you're forced to be in it. People can drag you into drama, commonly caused by problems with friends. There are exceptions where enemies can pull you into drama. Must be abused at home by a drunk father. Some people stand up to every fight they see. Those kids are like the main characters in a movie about them. They expect to be the center of attention. You could be inside a random drama right now, and you wouldn't know it! My friends and I are never in those dramas.

Sadly, we don't have the guts to save someone from getting bullied. But could you blame us? They will compel us if we protect them. I wouldn't even save someone. I would never have the guts to do that. Barely anybody would. Well, I will never have to decide to save someone. So much can change from one choice. Don't underestimate it.

If you're new, here's what I will tell you. Don't save anyone. Stay away from the bullies. Ignore them as best as you can. If they bully you, don't fight back. You'll just get blamed by the teachers.

Wait, one last tip:

Don't be a freak like me.

◆ ◆ ◆

I woke up from my aggravating alarm. I opened my eyes to see the plain white ceiling with peeling paint. After much self-encouragement, I got up from bed and went to my shiny bathroom to wash my face and teeth. The bathroom has walls that are all colored light yellow. It has a door that leads to the shower and toilet. I did not open the door as I didn't need to use the restroom. I went to the mirror, which was above my sink. I stared at myself and saw a face that would never be as attractive as Vanessa's. I quickly distracted myself and washed my face with clear water and liquid soap. When I finished, I returned to my simple bedroom to change clothes. Most people have those excruciatingly detailed bedrooms with everything possible inside them. When I was little, I used to ask Mom for a new bedroom. I was disappointed with my simple room. Do you want to know what my bedroom looks like? It has a wardrobe, a "bed" with no rim (more like a mattress) and a side table. That's it. These days, I am completely fine with it. I thought about what to wear today and found my favorite navy blue cargo pants and a white shirt. I don't like to spend too much time thinking about what to wear, so I put this on. People say that it's terrible for your health, or whatever.

 I walked down the stairs feeling cold. When I arrived downstairs, I smelled my Mom making my favorite breakfast, fried egg, sunny-side up. Mom looked exhausted, so I grabbed a cookie from the pantry and handed it to her. She must've had a night shift again from work. She smiled, and so did I. I walked away to the table I worked at and grabbed my phone to start playing a game. Don't we need our phones everywhere with us? I stopped when Mom shouted breakfast was ready. I grabbed my fried egg with ease. I walked back to the table. I sat down on my favored dining seat. While sitting down, I started to look out the window. It was when I finally realized there was snow! Snow is so rare here due to global warming. A smile lit up as I watched the whitest snow fall from the clouds. Looking there made me feel so nostalgic for my younger self. Isn't it the best feeling ever? To recall all those fun times you had as a child?

The table is filthy and has a dead plant in the middle. Mom avowed that she would get new plants soon and take care of them. As far as I know, Mom has never cared for the plants. To be fair, I forget to remind her to water them. But this time, I will remind her! *I hope.*

I started chowing down on the delicious egg. It is so satisfying to pop the yolk with a shiny metal fork. If you add seasoning, the taste is unbeatable.

After breakfast, I packed my marigold school bag and asked Mom to drive me there. She divulged that she could drive me, and we had to go outside to reach the car. I admired the even white snow and picked some up. I ruined the ground, making a hole in the field. I made an imperfect snowball and threw it on the snow. I walked on a brick pathway with orange and red bricks, which now had snow on top. We were walking to the car, and when we entered, I was hit with the weird car smell. I looked at the black leather seats with Mom holding her car keys. It felt lovely and relieving to see the outdoors. I'm glad I don't constantly stay inside my home.

"Mom, when are you coming home today?" I asked.

"By six. There are many patients today, so I will be late." Mom is a nephrologist.

"Alright. Is it okay there? Have any patients died?"

"There is one named Liv. She is sick, and I must try to care for her. She has kidney failure. We have to give her surgery, and it is perilous. I am afraid she will die, and I don't want to let her family down. All we can do is pray she will survive."

I shouldn't have asked that question. It made me feel sick in the stomach. Liv could've been a fantastic person, donating to people experiencing poverty and helping the environment. Due to her kidney failure, she is slowly losing her life. What can I do for her? Will she live?

When we arrived at school, I said goodbye to Mom and looked outside the building. I saw the same creepy, smooth, brown brick building with the giant automatic sliding doors. The school is trying to incorporate more modern technology. If you stand outside the door's entrance, then it opens automatically! Imagine you were entering a castle disguised as a jail. That's exactly how it feels. There are windows in every classroom except the ones on the inside. They all have these blue curtains with a chevron design on them. Everyone can't tell if the curtains are royal-blue or cobalt. The lights on the inside flicker and have bugs inside them. They give the lights a disco shine, with the bugs being opaque. The school is bigger than you could imagine. It has lockers on every single wall! I can feel the skies singing to me inside the school. I want to be outside, to be free! I want to sing to the songbirds and fly with the clouds! Just forget that the clouds are made of water! The walls are chalky and made of rusty white concrete. I saw my face cleanly reflected off the white tile floor. I walked inside and saw the group standing near the water fountain. They looked excited. Maybe they have something special in mind?

"Monica, have you heard? The school is finally adding new water fountains!" Chantelle exclaimed.

"Thank the lord, now half of them won't taste like toilet water," I cheered. Everyone started laughing. "Maybe they'll get a new lunch menu too?" I thought. I hope so. I dislike lunch food from my public high school. Ah, classic Willow Creek. Imagine putting the "food" into a trash can. That is a pitch-perfect representation of the taste of lunch food.

I grabbed a book from my locker when I saw Vanessa walking down the hallway with Grant. She announced a few days ago that they were dating. Based on my knowledge, he's just a geeky kid. He isn't that attractive, but I would expect someone like her to have higher standards. He has an affectionate soul. Souls like that don't have the best chances of surviving high school. I was confident she would date Bradley, one of the prominent jocks.

I went to grab the rest of my books and noticed how all the girls were watching Vanessa in awe. They see beauty; I see manipulation. Maybe I'm just being paranoid. Am I?

"That's, like, the third person she has dated this month," Alexandra uttered.

"I know. What if Vanessa has a secret?" I thought, why am I always thinking of her?

"Ring, Ring!" That's the bell. We have to get to class. I was walking the loud, cluttered school halls to get to class. I already had all my books, so I didn't need to worry about forgetting anything. Thank god I am not a forgetful person.

When we arrived at class, I saw Mrs. Hamlet, the language arts teacher. She was standing at the door, waiting for everyone to come. I once again smelled the classroom smell and looked around it. The classroom had a cluttered fashion and tiled walls. All language arts classrooms here have a stereotype of being messy. There is a theory here that Mrs. Hamlet became a language arts teacher because of her name. Hamlet is a story by William Shakespeare. The blinds were closed, and the blocked light made the classroom darker despite the lights being turned on. There were stacks of books, mainly composed of famous classics. A few cabinets consisted of books. The school curriculum has a book club, but I dislike it. Mrs. Hamlet gives us a bucket load of homework regarding book club. Thankfully, we don't have to read boring books this semester. I like reading, but even I dislike those books. They are worded so weirdly that it confuses me!

 I sat at my desk and looked around while other kids came in. By 8 a.m., language arts started.

 "Alright, class, today we will get a pop quiz!" Mrs. Hamlet announced cheerfully.

 I groaned. Of course, we got a pop quiz. That's the average Willow Creek teacher! I waited for the teacher to give me a test. The glee on her face meant she enjoyed sharing the test, which let us students down. One of the main reasons I dislike high school is because of pop quizzes. Like, come on! Tell us when we're having a quiz. Come on, don't be shy. What did all these students (including me) do to deserve this?

When I got my test, I saw the class clown bullying a fellow nerd. I took a deep breath, thankful everyone had forgotten about me.

I started taking the quiz and realized how easy it was. I expected it to be difficult since Mrs. Hamlet makes complex tests, but this was one of the most straightforward tests I've ever taken. There were 25 questions, and I finished them in at max 10 minutes. Mrs. Hamlet grades tests the same day you receive them. I got 25/25. It was the easiest test ever!

When we had no more time for the quiz, she gave us a lesson, and when she finished the lesson, we left. I sat with my friends at lunch and talked about the quiz.

"That was, like, the easiest pop quiz I've ever taken," I shared.

"I know! I finished it in, like, two minutes," Alexandra announced.

"Same."

We didn't talk much more, and I don't know why. I guess we wanted to eat our delicious lunches, which were *not* from the school cafeteria.

After school, I went home and hoped Mom was

there. I walked in, screaming Mom. She wasn't here, and I wasn't surprised. She's always at work, prioritizing it more than anything. I took my phone and started watching social media. I decided to watch a baking video. Mom is always at work, so I figured making her some food would be an excellent surprise. I wanted to find out what to make and decided on vanilla cake. I prefer chocolate cake, but Mom says she isn't a big chocolate fan. I looked for a recipe online and found one that was flawless.

    I could smell how marvelous it was when we got it out of the oven. I found mittens in a white drawer and took them out. I prayed it wouldn't stick to the pan. I flipped over the pan, slammed the bottom a few times, and shook it. However, the cake stuck to the pan, so my hope was lost. I cut the cake evenly and found a small plate. I placed a piece of cake on the plate. I melted a piece of chocolate and got some sprinkles from the pantry. I put some whipped cream on the thick part of the cake to add flair. I also added some strawberries to dip in the melted chocolate. It smelled scrumptious, and I wanted to eat her slice. I didn't feel like making another slice, so I resisted the urge to take a bite. I got my phone and scrolled on my phone while sitting at the table, waiting for Mom. But after a few hours, Mom didn't come home. She told me in the morning that she would be home by six, but the clock struck eight. I tried to call her, but she didn't accept. It went to voicemail.

Now I'm worried. But Mom probably has extra patients. She will come home soon. I should wrap the cake up now that I think about it. Can cakes rot in the first place? I don't know, but it shouldn't sit on the counter. I put a plate on top of the cake. Now it won't spoil. Sadly, the sweet cake aroma is gone. Now I want a snack. I entered the pantry and grabbed a granola bar. I ate it and started to scroll on my phone and wait. How fun.

After a tiresome two-hour wait, she finally came home. When she was at the door, I hugged her like never before. It isn't typical for Mom to make me wait for this long. Where was she?

"Monica, I am so sorry I am so late," Mom muttered. I could see her look of worry. She must've been terrified about coming home late because she thought I would panic. I did panic, but not on the level of calling the police like a little kid. Mom looked so disheartened in herself. I wish she would know that it's okay.

"Mom, it's okay that you came late. I didn't do anything extreme that little kids would do. I just got a little worried. I made you a cake hours ago." I winked and gave Mom my cake. She was so thrilled, and she hugged me extremely hard. She tasted the cake and immediately looked shunned. She smiled at me, saying it was delicious. She told me that she still had tons of work to do, so she sat on the couch to do it. I was drained, so I went to bed upstairs and slept. I walked up the evenly shaped wooden stairs. I strutted to my room. As I was in my bed, I felt appeased. Doing deeds for my parents made me feel affectionate. I guess we have to help our parents at least occasionally. Helping them makes them feel proud of you as if you didn't forget them. It makes you feel positive as well. Of course, it makes you feel wonderful. You helped someone. Unless you were an evil villain, then you would feel horrible.

I closed my eyes and wondered what was happening with other people's lives. I knew some people were less fortunate. I felt lucky to be in my home, sleeping in a bed. I looked around my dull room when I could hear Mom coming upstairs. Wasn't Mom doing work five minutes ago? I looked at my alarm clock, and it was 11:30. I was shocked I couldn't sleep for this long. Time flies by that fast? Does Mom work for this long? What is happening?

✧ ✧ ✧

The next day was chaotic. When I arrived at school, I met my friends and talked about a bad kid named Connor. He is a trendy kid, but he bullies a ton of people. At 11 a.m., we had math, and our math teacher was named Mr. Leslie. He introduced something vital.

"Class, I have something crucial to tell you," Mr. Leslie announced.

"Who cares?" A kid called out.

"You will care because we are having our math final on Friday!" Mr. Leslie had an evil smirk. "This test is essential, especially since it is worth 10% of your grade." Oh man, Mr. Leslies' tests are challenging. I raised my hand.

"Will the test be timed?" I asked.

"Yes, you will have an hour to finish it."

So, timed tests are my biggest weakness. I am the slowest test-taker in the class. I am talking about international math problems. A few hours of studying could do the trick. Isn't studying fun?

We did math practice for the remainder of the class. Bradley and Chad would probably cease to function, wondering what to do. For the rest of the class, I planned strategies to use on the test. If I couldn't solve the question, I would move on to a different one. Self-encouragement wasn't a pain.

At noon, we went to lunch. It smelled horrible, like the average school lunchroom. The floors were so dirty, with food all over them. I don't think the custodians thoroughly clean the floor. They may pick up food there, but I don't believe it when they say they wipe the floor with a mop.

After Grant became Vanessa's boyfriend, his popularity skyrocketed. All the "cool kids" are sitting with him, like Bradley, Chad, and, of course, Connor. Connor might be losing popularity due to the kids he is bullying. People are starting to stay away from him. That's excellent. I could see all the girls staring at Vanessa. She was talking with her best friend, Ester. I consider her to be my polar opposite. Ester always considers herself the best girl in school, and I think she wants to be more popular than Vanessa. The whole school knows that Ester is jealous of Vanessa. I'm surprised Vanessa hasn't realized Ester's devilish acts.

I looked at Sheldon (a nerd) and saw Connor using a straw to make spitballs. Every day, he would throw spitballs in Sheldon's hair. The tiny wet paper towel would go inside the straw and fly to his thin, soiled locks. Bradley and Chad were laughing with Connor, but Grant seemed reluctant. He has a good soul, unwilling to hurt anyone.

Onto another topic, Sheldon looks done. He didn't look pleased. It was like he had a sly grin under those square glasses. They have bullied him since the start of middle school. The funny thing is, Sheldon has always had this notebook with him. It seems weird to have a notebook, especially with the bullies constantly nagging him. It must be a diary, and students could read it out loud.

Then, I saw it. My eyes didn't believe what they saw.

Sheldon was holding a tray full of chocolate milk.

He spilled it all over Connor!

Connor looked angry and bugged. He couldn't take it. He slowly turned his head and stared at Sheldon with gritted teeth. His eyes were shot open, and his shirt was darker from the spill. Connor chuckled, unable to believe what happened. He is a jock with blonde hair and blue eyes, the classic. He wore a red jacket with a white shirt underneath. You know those vests that represent the school football team? He constantly wore that jacket. His white shirt was ruined with that stain. That clean white now had a tint of dark brown. Connor curled his fist and started to chase him. Sheldon, with his weak legs, struggled to run away.

"Fight!" Someone shouted.

"Yeah, fight!" Another person shouted.

Soon, everyone was chanting fight! Vanessa was excessively passionate about the fight. Connor was about to punch Sheldon, but he dodged.

"Stop bullying others just because of your problems with home," Sheldon calmly shared. He took a deep breath, knowing Connor was going to attempt to kill him.

"Oooh," everybody murmured. Oh man, Connor got burned! Sheldon crumpled his eyebrows with a smirk, which made Connor angry. I could not imagine being in that position.

"Shut up! That is not true!" His voice trailed off quietly. He was about to lay a punch on Sheldon. He tried to punch him, but Sheldon dodged and kicked him in the ribs.

"Help!" Connor shouted. He was on the ground and looked like he was about to cry. Well, he did cry. Everyone was laughing. He was sure to get a nickname.

"Hey, guys! His nickname should be Crying Connor!" One person shouted.

"Yeah! Let's call him that!" Another person shouted.

Now, everyone was chanting and calling him Crying Connor. He got a taste of ugly alliteration. He will not survive the next year of high school. I wish him luck, but he is guaranteed to die. Chad and Bradley will dump him due to their popularity. However, I don't know about Grant. He will probably try to save him. After all, he has a good soul. I feel like Connor is lucky that Grant is here. He most likely will try to save him. But will Grant sacrifice his popularity? I have no idea.

Great. Another jock lost all they had.

I have to take the school bus home. It is a dreadful experience. As a student who is one of the last stops, I have to wait for hours to get home, and I envy the kids who get to go home first. They have it so easy, and we last students have it hard. The worst part is the bus driver makes the "cool kids" go home last as a punishment! I have to hear their bickering for hours. I can listen to all their gossip. I get to hear their opinions. I don't want to listen to it! What did I do to deserve this in the first place? I am fourth last, and I must stay with them for that long! Luckily, they ignored me since I sat at the best spot on the bus. Back-middle. The back is for all the "cool kids." Everyone forgets the back middle. Too many students sit in the middle, making it unreasonably crowded. Even though it is deafening to be near the back, it's easy to ignore. Besides, the front is the worst place. Everybody would think of you as a chicken scared of the cool kids. Trust me, I have experience.

When I finished class, I was stuck with a crowd of kids running to go home. Everybody wants to go home to get out of this weird dump. It makes sense but isn't enjoyable since you're trying to get through. Leaving the school takes a few minutes, but you can eventually pass. Everybody was screaming to get out of school, and I stayed calm, saying nothing. When I finally got out, I went on my bus and sat at seat 16. Not too close to the back, not too far away from it. Today, Connor was the last person to enter the bus—which wasn't even a surprise. Everybody started laughing at him. When he went to the back, Bradley and Chad kicked him out.

"I couldn't imagine losing a fight to Sheldon!" One person shouted.

"Yeah! He's, like, the weakest person in school."

"Shut up!" Connor shouted.

I could see his embarrassment. We all could.

Connor went to seat 17 on the bus, right across from me. I didn't want to talk to him, so I just got my favorite book out and started reading. It's a bit disheartening that he is sitting here. From the corner of my eye, I saw Connor staring at me. Why? He must be thinking about my looks. Wait, he probably forgot that I exist. Does he think I'm a new student? Just focus on reading. Focus,

focus, focus. There's no way he wants to talk to me in the first place.

"Hey, uhh, you're that Monica girl, right?" He asked.

"Uh, yeah, that's my name," I answered.

"Cool, I heard you're like, brilliant."

"I'm kind of smart, I guess," I replied.

"I know this is a weird question, but, like, can you help me get my popularity? Maybe you could help me become more intelligent as well?"

"Hmm, maybe."

✧ Chapter Two ✧

Why, out of all people, did he ask me to help him!? I am not a good person for this! Like, have you even seen my reputation? I can't just decline his request, either! He's going to think of me as a cruel, useless person! I don't want to be thought of as a loser! This isn't good. I might sacrifice the status that I worked so hard for to help him. I can't ruin it! I have one more insipid year of high school. One more insipid year of torture. I will not be able to survive that with a ruined status due to bullies. I have no idea what I should do. This is bad. Really bad. Oh gosh. I panicked for a while until I came home. I saw

Mom cooking. I was taken aback by surprise when I saw what she was cooking.

"Mom, you're making duck confit?" I was shocked. Duck confit takes hours, so I have no idea how Mom even had the time to make it!

"How did you make it? You never have time for this!" My shock was visible to Mom. Duck confit is a French dish. You must cure duck legs overnight before you submerge the legs in duck fat. Then, gently cook it until it is tender. I can't remember the last time Mom made this. It is my favorite dish to this day. She commonly made it when I was younger, but not as much anymore. It warms my heart to see that Mom remembers my younger self.

"While you were asleep, I decided to make you duck confit. I knew you liked it, and you made me that delicious cake! I had to return the favor. In fact, it is almost done!"

"Thank you so much!" I smiled. I rarely get to have it, so hearing Mom spent her free time making it for me instead of resting made me smile. This explains why she was awake for so long last night.

"Tell me when you finish it because I have a lot of work today. I will be working at the dining table."

"Alright," Mom sighed.

I have to study for the test. You heard Mr. Leslie. He proclaimed it was worth 10 percent of my grade. Based on my first-quarter grade, I got an A *minus*. This test could save my grade and jump it to a full A. I have to study my best, and Mom called me for dinner an hour later. I walked over there, and I could smell the fresh duck smell. I was so enthusiastic I was going to jump up and down. It was like being a baby receiving a giant rainbow lollipop. With every step I took, my excitement got higher and higher. As I got closer and closer, I felt like I was about to scream! Finally, I get to have the food I have wanted for years! When I finally arrived at the kitchen, Mom had prepared some food. She gave it to me in a bowl. I went to the dining table and stared at it for a minute. It looked mouth-watering. Then, I dug in. It was the most delicious thing I've ever tasted! Let me tell you, it was fit for a king! Every flavor ever to exist exploded in my mouth, and it made me feel harmonious. Not only that, but it looked appealing as well.

I studied for three hours. That's how nervous I am. I am still agitated and have to pray I don't mess up. It was 10 p.m., so I decided to go to sleep.

As I was in bed, I thought of Connor. He was so popular and lost all of his popularity in a second. It is so unfortunate for that to happen to someone. Will that happen to me? Will I lose all I have worked for? I don't know, but I need to try to avoid it. Just stay in the shadows, Monica, remain in the shadows.

The next day, I prepared for school and went downstairs for breakfast. I saw Mom making two fried eggs again, which delighted me. One for her and one for me. Mom finished making the dish, so I took it to the dining table. I dug in, and when I finished breakfast, I went into Mom's car to get to school. I was walking there and could see the frost on the car windows. When I got inside the car, I saw the black leather seats. The seats were ripped, and the car didn't smell too good. I have always been worried that it made us look poor. You don't want to look poor in high school, especially in Willow Creek.

I looked out the window and saw the outside world. I saw my street name and the sign for 20 miles per hour.

When we arrived at school the next day, I looked for my friends and wanted to talk to them. I saw the crowd of kids trying to go inside. I needed to tell them about Connor and what he said yesterday. When I passed the crowd of students, I saw Connor getting bullied. I went past him, and I think he didn't notice. I went to my friends and saw them talking near my locker.

"Hey guys, have you seen what happened to Connor?" I asked.

"Man, I don't feel a pinch of sympathy for him. He bullied so many kids that it was bound to get to him eventually. It's called karma," Alexandra joked.

"Haha, true. You know, Vanessa was supporting the fight. Sadly, nobody even heard a word from her."

"Not going to lie, but you're always talking about Vanessa. It's not like she's the most important person to exist," Chantelle pointed out.

"Chantelle's kinda right," Eloise agreed. "You're always talking about her. I thought you didn't care about her."

"I don't, but she is suspicious. Nobody can be so flawless."

"Yeah, but you don't always have to talk about Vanessa. We can have a conversation without mentioning her."

"I guess you're right," I'll say to them. This conversation doesn't change my opinion of her. Something's up.

At math, we were preparing for the test tomorrow. I kept studying with my math textbook and looking through my notes. I grabbed some of the practice papers to do. I could see how worried some students were.

Judging by Mr. Leslies' usual curriculum, there will be problems in the test from the practice pages. He will switch the numbers in the questions to ensure we don't remember the old answer. I should memorize these questions so I know the process to solve them. That's what a wise person would do.

As I was studying, some students weren't even bothering to look in their notebooks. They were playing a game on their phone and using their notebooks to cover it. They stuck a notebook up like a privacy shield and used their phones. How clever and cheap. I did the practice problems, and someone tapped my shoulder. Guess who it was? Connor.

"Hey, hey! Could you help me with this?" He asked.

He's talking to me. I have to play sharp.

"Why are you asking me to help you?"

"You just seem like the perfect person. You are elegant and clever. You could help me become the best of the best." He is good at reasoning. I don't think you should describe me as elegant. Yeah, I don't know what I was thinking at that moment. Why did I become so cunning? I have to help him now. Will I get service hours from this?

"Acceptable reasoning, but it can be better. I'll help

you," I gave in.

"Thank you so much!"

"Don't mention it. Now, first, we have to solve the brackets." I taught him how to do equations, more specifically, the order of operations. To be honest, he wasn't too dumb compared to other people. He just needed a little work and a push. I am thankful he was paying attention. I tutored other kids for extra credit, and they never paid attention. He is interested to learn.

After math and lunch, it was time for a debate class, gym. Some people love it, and some people hate it. We can all agree that it is controversial.

Going into the gym, I could tell how unfortunate this would be. The teacher looked around the gym, waiting for the kids to enter. He gets frustrated when students are late. Once everybody was here, he gave us our classic lesson, dodgeball. There was a black bin full of balls, and he dumped them out on the floor. He put them all near the middle and made us play rock-paper-scissors to determine which team we'd be on. If you win, you get team one. If you lose, you get team two. Nobody was coming to me, so I decided to go on team one. Once everyone got their teams, we started the game. Everybody started shouting immediately! People are competitive during these games, even though it isn't the most important thing ever.

Everyone threw ball after ball, and I was among the last girls out. People were constantly getting hit by balls, and the score ended at three-one. Connor against Chad, Bradley, and Drew. Drew is a popular kid whom all the girls like. All the girls were cheering for him.

This last part of the game was tense. Connor got Chad out of the game, but Bradley and Drew were still in. Chad has brown hair and multi-colored eyes. (Heterochromia.) One eye is brown, and one is green. He is always blabbering about his heterochromia. Connor was intensely sweating. Drew had a malicious simper on his face. Drew threw the ball with force and hit Connor in the face. He was out. His cheek had a red spot. He put his hand on his cheek. Connor must've felt bad, so I felt like being a human. I went over to him to cheer him up, to remove that frown from his face.

"Hey Connor, most people don't even get one person out in a three-verse-one! You should be proud of yourself! Are you okay?"

"Yeah, I'm fine. Can anyone see my bruise?"

"Nah, not really."

"Anyway, thank you. When this stuff happens, nobody asks if I'm okay. You must be the first one to be considerate of me!"

"Oh, aha, thanks."

Everyone chanted Drew's name. He is more attractive and robust than Chad and Bradley combined. Drew has brown hair and green eyes. People love him mainly because he is athletic—always being the best in every sport. Chad and Bradley hate him but are afraid to admit it.

When school finished and I was home, I took a deep breath—the last day before the test. I have to take it cautiously. Minute after minute, thoughts of anxiety were coming into my mind. I felt worried and afraid to get a lousy grade. Teachers can post everyone's grades on a board. If I get one lousy score, my reputation will be destroyed. Everyone will think that I'm dumb. That I faked being so bright. Everyone would assume I'm a liar despite their no idea about my life. They would think that I bribed someone to give me good grades. People love to make up a random excuse and blame people for it.

I studied for a few hours and later wrote a letter to myself.

I know it sounds weird, but I like to write letters to remind me what to do, what tricks to use, and what will help me get the top score. The tricks you use depend on the subject and type of test. This technique could help your grades improve! I pull the letter out right before the test and skim through it. I hide it from the teachers so they don't assume I'm cheating.

Dear Monica,

I'm writing this for your test tomorrow. I didn't want to break the tradition. Here are tips that will hopefully help you do well. Remember that this test is timed!

Don't be stupid. Don't make dumb mistakes. Show as much work as you can. You can get extra credit for doing that. Don't spend too much time showing your work! Check your work. You will get at least three wrong if you don't check your work. Don't check it for too long!

Most importantly, answer the questions first and then check it!

Kids who finish their tests fast fail the test. Be fast, but don't finish it in five minutes.

Last but not least, don't be dreadful on the test. You will severely regret it.

To Monica, a questionable person.

I folded the lined paper in half. I went to my school bag and put it in my main pocket. I felt at ease that I got everything done. I felt oddly tired, so I went to bed for a good night's rest. I stared at my bland ceiling and just thought about my life. It could be much worse. I am the victim, and I shouldn't tell anyone about it. I know Vanessa is evil. Screw telling my friends, they'll criticize me. Everyone will attack me for a year. Why am I so miserable now? Why can't I have my old life back? Will anything change since I'm with Connor? Why are there so many things that could happen? All these questions; I must be a goner. I shouldn't just leave my old life away. I am a loser. I stay away from everyone. I will try to get my life back. No, not try. I *will* get my life back!

◆ ◆ ◆

The next day, I woke up and tried to set my alarm to snooze. I was dreading going to school today. But after a few minutes, I decided to get up and deal with it. I went to the bathroom to brush my teeth. I wet the toothbrush and put a glob of toothpaste on it. I put the toothbrush in my mouth and scrubbed it hard. It felt revolting. When I finished brushing my teeth, I spit the toothpaste out. I put water in my mouth and spit it out to get the minty taste out. It was still there. After some grumbling, I went to wash my face. I could feel the relieving feeling of your face being cleansed. When I finished my skincare, I went to my closet to change. I decided to wear emerald green cargo pants with a black shirt. The pants had a small stain, but I could deal with it. I went to change my flower earrings to these lock-and-key earrings. I felt like it represented this chapter of my life. I'm locking up the old one and opening a new one with a key. I looked in the mirror to make sure my earrings were on correctly. I also had to move my necklace to put the charm on the front. When I finished, I looked at my bland room with its boring yellow walls.

I left the room and walked down the hallway to the stairs. I could feel the nice cold touch of the wooden railing. While going downstairs, I could smell Mom's delicious breakfast. Thank god for her.

When I arrived, Mom handed me breakfast. She looked weirdly tired, and I think I know why.

"Mom, were you on call yesterday?" I asked.

"Yep."

"Oh man, I'm sorry." When Mom is on call, she has to stay up the whole night to ensure her patient doesn't call her. It's outrageous! The patients would be incredibly rude and stupid to call her late at night. Why would they do that in the first place? Wouldn't they be sleeping in their hospital bed?

"Will you go to work today?"

"Sadly," she was so tired, I felt so bad.

"I won't disturb you for the rest of the day. Will that make you feel good?"

"What? No! Every time I see you, I feel my day becoming better."

"Thank you, Mom," she flattered me. I left just to realize the test was today! I can't believe I forgot! I was about to panic, but I couldn't stress out Mom. I calmed down and didn't tell Mom to take me to school. If she drove me to school tired, then she could easily crash. I don't want to die. I'm only 17. For me and her, I decided to take the worst place imaginable, the bus. I hoped nobody would sit in my seat when I got on the bus.

To my surprise, Connor was sitting there. That is my favorite seat, so I softly groaned. I have to help Connor, so why not sit with him?

"Hey, Connor. Do you feel prepared for the test? I hope I prepared you well."

But then, he immediately hugged me.

"You are such a compassionate person. Different from what I've seen, at least."

"Thank you." I was surprised he would be so thankful. If he needed that much help, wouldn't he ask his parents to help him? Maybe something happened at home. I probably shouldn't assume that. "Why are you hugging me? I probably didn't even teach you that well. I'm not that good of a teacher."

"Are you kidding? You're the best teacher! I learned so quickly from you. I've never been more confident for a test!"

"Thanks. Would you like me to give you more lessons?"

"Of course! Thank you."

That conversation made me feel satisfied. Never in my life has someone been so thankful to me. Maybe I should help him more. It would do more good than bad for me. Wait a moment, wouldn't this affect my status at school? You know what? I was paranoid yesterday. This won't be a huge deal. I decided to test him on more math, and he quickly answered all the questions. I have a good feeling for him. He will pass the test for sure. I could hear the "cool kids" screaming in the back. It made me want to jump off the bus.

When the bus arrived at school, I was the first to get off. I ran, skipping through a few seats to go to the front. Everyone was aware of what I did. Besides, who wants to get off last in that dump?

In all the other classes before math, I secretly studied. I put the notebook beneath all my work, and not a single teacher noticed. After all, being such a prestigious student can have its advantages.

Once math started, Mr. Leslie asked everyone to turn in their homework. To my surprise, Connor and I were the only kids to complete their homework. Mr. Leslie approached me and Connor. He gave us a high-five. I was amused, as this would be something I wouldn't forget for today. We were both shocked, but I will assume that everyone else was studying late. They completely forgot about the homework. One thing: Mr. Leslie *hates* students who don't do their homework. His face was fuming, and a joyful idea came to his head. He gave us extra credit for the test. It delighted me, but I could still fail, so I shouldn't get my hopes too high.

He gave everyone a lecture to do the homework. After that boring lecture, Mr. Leslie finally started to pass out the test. He clearly emphasized that we couldn't begin until he started the timer. I was looking frantically through the questions. There were 25 questions, and we had an hour. I divided 60 by 25, and I got 2.4. So that means I have to spend two minutes and 40 seconds on one question. That's more than enough. He had the timer on the projector, which was a disadvantage for me. I stress when I see the time. I read the note I wrote and put it in my pocket. I knew what to do.

"Start!" He shouted.

The test was difficult. But overall, I was able to do it. Every problem made me think outside the box, but I was able to solve it. Halfway through the assessment, I could see someone looking in my direction. Their eyes wandered onto my test answers. I felt a little panicked. Why is someone cheating off me? Has this happened before, but I didn't notice? Is this happening since I'm helping Connor? It was someone behind me, so I turned around and saw it was Bradley. He turned his head and focused on his test. He was tapping his pencil instead of writing. I knew he was stupid, but he's a rotten cheater. If you want to cheat off me, then you have to work better than that. I will realize it eventually. I wanted to laugh, but everyone would hear me, so I just did a slight chuckle. It was loud enough for him to hear. How long has he been doing this? When I finished the test, I turned it in. I only had three minutes left, so I felt proud. Usually, I end the test with 20 seconds remaining. I have to run to turn it in. Today was my lucky day. I wanted to pat myself on the back.

Mr. Leslie, like Mrs. Hamlet, grades the tests the same day we get them. He also announces the three kids who got the highest scores. Most of the time, I get number one. I hope I'll get it this time. I started reading my book when the timer started to beep. Some kids jumped out of their chairs. Everyone turned in their test. After some grading, he found everyone's scores. I then saw no point in reading when we had three minutes. Why was I doing that?

"I have the highest scores on the test here. I will let you think about the kids with the highest scores." Everyone was silent. They were wondering who got the highest scores.

"The person who got the highest score was," he paused for a dramatic silence. "Connor!"

I jumped. I was incredibly proud of him. I will admit I am a little dismayed about getting lower than first, but I guess it's okay. I hope I get second.

"The person who got the second highest score was," he paused again. "Monica!" I guess my studying was worth it. If I taught Connor that well, then I must be excellent at mathematics. You have to study, and you will get good grades. It's shocking how so many people don't understand that. Some kids think learning doesn't work and getting good grades is only for talented kids. I have never seen something so wrong. I went to Connor and talked to him.

"Connor, good job!" I never thought he would get

such a good score.

"Thanks to my amazing teacher," he winked at me. He left, and I started to approach my friends. I saw them talking near my locker once again. I walked over there from the clear school floor. When I arrived, we started talking.

"Let's go to lunch!" I felt excited.

"Yeah, let's talk on the way there," Chantelle responded.

"How did you do on the math test?" I immediately asked.

"I got 92. How about you?" Chantelle felt pride.

"I got 96," I responded.

"I got 71," Alexandra quietly confessed. It felt like she was disappointed with her score.

"I got 100." Eloise softly pointed out. Her voice was plump and soft.

"Wow, that's amazing, Eloise!" I exclaimed. "You're brilliant at math! Like a god! You know what? From now on, I'll call you Eloise, the math god!" We started chanting Eloise's name. Getting 100 is impressive, especially from a test by Mr. Leslie. His tests have a ton of wordplay, so most kids get at least one question wrong because they read it wrong. It is so galling. We must learn to read the question carefully because "we will need to identify tricky wordplay in college."

When we arrived at the lunchroom, I could smell lousy food on the floor. You can smell the disgusting lunch food when you enter. Kids were screaming. There were people wasting straws for spitballs, basically the average lunchroom. It's funny since the custodians have displayed multiple notes saying "save the turtles" around the straw cans.

We looked around to find empty seats for the four of us. We found some, but these other kids wanted them. We ran to the accessible seats. We got them, but those kids stared at us weirdly. We started to laugh, and then we talked.

I started eating my lunch, and then I heard a splash. I heard a loud groan. I was a little confused, so I turned my head and saw it.

Someone had thrown an apple at Sheldon's head!

You won't believe who threw it. The person I believed wouldn't change, Grant. I never expected this to happen. He had such a cordial heart, and I thought he wouldn't hurt a fly. My friends, this is what popularity does to you. It can twist the kindest, most loving souls into disgusting, wicked evil. I stared in shock, and guess what had come in? No other than Vanessa.

"Grant, why would you hit him!?" Vanessa shouted.

"It's fine. Just deal with Grant hitting me due to his despair," Sheldon weakly mumbled. He was so puny that he could barely speak.

"I-I didn't mean to hit him! I swear I meant to hit Connor!" Grant begged.

"Connor is understandable, but him?" She yelled. "That's it, Grant! I am done dating you!" She shouted. Nobody bawled an ooh or aah. We all knew Grant was done in the first week.

They're all done in the first week.

But seriously, why did he even throw that apple in the first place? Throwing an apple at someone's head is not a good deed, and I'm pretty sure your parents wouldn't want you to do that.

Do you want to know the worst part of all?

A week later, Vanessa started dating Drew. Again.

I left the scene to begin reading. Slowly, other people started leaving as well. This scene was going to be the highlight of gossip. I know she is the leader of it. She tries not to show it, but the whole school knows. Weeks ago, I was getting books out of my locker, and she discussed these two kids dating. She acts so "innocent" while being the leader of it all. How is someone so messed up? I went on the bus to get home.

When I arrived home, I asked Mom if she was okay. She tiredly addressed that she was sleepy. I didn't have much homework, so I went to the couch to watch television when I finished it. I decided to watch one of my favorite dramas. I love drama like Mom. It is entertaining to watch. I could stare at it for hours! I guess I love to see people suffer. Who doesn't?

After a fun time staring at shouting, I went to sleep.

✧ ✧ ✧

The next day at school, I was met with a surprise. Bradley and Chad didn't kick out Grant. They wanted to keep him badly as a part of the friend group. He surprised them by trying to hurt someone in the first place. Oh, this is weird.

I went to Chantelle and Eloise, but Alexandra wasn't there.

"Where's Alexandra?" I asked.

"We don't know."

"I'll call her. I also have to use the bathroom, so I'll see you in a minute." I left to go to the bathroom. I decided to call her on the way.

"Ring ring!" My phone was ringing. It took a few seconds, but Alexandra accepted my call.

"Hey, Alexandra! I wanted to check up on you to

see if you were okay. Are you sick?"

"M-Monica, I need to t-tell you something."

"Yes?"

"Ester p-punched me yesterday. She left a n-note as w-well. It said she w-was,"

"Was what!?"

"W-was coming for m-me."

◈ Chapter Three ◈

How does she get school off from getting bullied? How could Ester target someone so innocent? Alexandra didn't do a thing to her. What should I do? Should I help Alexandra, or should I stay in the shadows? If I help her, I will bring attention to myself, and god knows what can happen. If I don't help her, then I am a horrible person. I have to help her, right? Choosing is so hard. But maybe I could cheat my way out of it. After school, I decided to go to Alexandra's home. I needed to ask her questions. Right now, I have so many. At home, I told Mom what happened. She felt sympathy for her unfortune. Immediately, she grabbed these jam cookies from the pantry and told me to give them to her. Bless Mom's soul. I agreed and went outside to walk to her home. Our homes are close to each other. Although, it wasn't the best decision to go in this freezing weather. The cold breeze of wind went on my face. There were no leaves on the trees, and the bears were hibernating. The local pond was completely frozen. We needed to examine puddle water for science, but everything was frozen. It was snowing. I was freezing, but I needed to contact Alexandra to tell her I was coming. I grabbed my phone, and my shaky hand tried to call her. However, my fingers weren't cooperating, so I dropped my phone in the snow.

Coming to people's houses without saying anything is rude, but this was an emergency. I hope her parents don't think terrible things about me. I care about my friend's safety.

Walking there, I looked around at the plain trees with no leaves. All the leaves were on the ground, buried in the snow. The bare trees were like someone losing their hair. I looked around, grabbed some snow, and made a snowball. I angrily threw it on the concrete and shed a tear. My friends saved me from middle school bullies, and now, one of them is a victim in high school, which is ten times worse! I must help her, even if it ruins my status. It's like girl code.

When I arrived outside her home, I could see the red bricks around her house. The house was covered with snow, and the rim of her roof had icicles. I have memories of licking icicles. They were traumatizing. The rooftop was niveous, and I couldn't see the whole roof. The plants were so submerged in snow that they looked dispirited, like their feelings had been murdered. Nobody listened to them, and they lost it. The windows had a slight black tint, and some had their blinds closed. I didn't have a satisfying feeling, so I eerily approached. I took these wooden steps to enter. They had the loudest creaks. I looked at the doormat, and it warmly welcomed me.

"Ring!" The doorbell rang. I took a few steps back and took a deep breath.

"Oh, hello, Monica. How are you feeling today?"

"I feel well. Is Alexandra okay?" I asked.

"Oh yes, she's okay."

"We got some jam cookies for her. May I see her?" I asked eagerly. I want to ask questions: what was her experience like?

"Of course! Alexandra, come down here!" She yelled. "Thank you for the cookies."

"No problem!" I breathed and looked at the glazed floor to wait. I don't have the best eye contact. Her parents were sympathetic, and they would understand if anything happened. I wouldn't be surprised if Alexandra told her parents about what happened. That could be why they could stay home. If I told Mom, she would still force me to go to school. She would say I'm being paranoid, and I'll be fine. When Alexandra arrived, she looked horrible. Her eyes were extremely red, and her hair looked like Mom's in the morning. She was still wearing pajamas and kept looking over to the side. I knew she didn't wash her face in the morning. Her breath was stinky, so she didn't brush her teeth. Tsk, tsk, tsk. She looked like a messed-up antagonist from a movie.

I walked inside and asked if I could talk to her in private. I didn't want her parents to make a scene if they found out. If they did, they would go to school and tell the principal. Then, she would be an even bigger target. She agreed, and we went upstairs to her bedroom. It was a *mess*! It is possibly the messiest I've ever seen. There were dirty clothes and hangers all over the floor and a laundry basket in the corner of the room. She had a side table, and it was so messy! There was nail polish, skincare items, and books all on top of a storage desk.

She didn't even organize them. It was dusty, with some tiny spider webs in the corner. She had a bookshelf that had three books at most. Three! Why would you even get a bookshelf if you don't put any books on it? All it had was plants and makeup. What a waste of money.

"Hey, Alexandra, how are you doing?" I asked.

She didn't respond. She just looked at the floor. I think I heard a snicker. What's happening?

I waited a minute for a response, but she blurted nothing.

"Alexandra, are you okay?" I was worried, looking at her with terror. I was like a red crayon in a box of blue crayons.

"Haha, I pranked you! I can't believe you actually fell for that. Like, did you really think Ester punched me? You're so naïve. You know, Chantelle and Eloise were in on the trick. They thought they were being too obvious. Like, imagine falling for such a poorly crafted trick." She was laughing hysterically. You could see my face of despair and utter shock.

What the hell!?

"Why would you do that? I was genuinely worried. My mom even gave some of our cookies to you!" I felt so despondent. I wanted to smash something!

"It's just a prank. Like, jeez," I was furious. I

stomped my foot on the floor and ran downstairs. I flew outside the door and started running. How could someone do something like that!? I started running back home and didn't care about my shoes getting wet from the snow. Not only that, but it was rude of her to say something like that about Ester. I understand she wants to take over Vanessa, but I don't think she would turn to bullying! Well, maybe she would. The weather was freezing, and I struggled to walk, but I kept going. The iridescence of the moon shone on me. I got into the center of this. But that didn't even come into my mind. I wanted to stay as far away as possible from her home. I don't want to see her ugly, deformed face again. I started to get cold and tried to run. I was freezing! My whole face was frozen from the cold. I couldn't move any facial features on my face. My fingers were frozen shut. I tried rubbing my hands together, but that didn't help at all.

 Once I saw my home, I went inside as fast as possible. My house had icicles on the rim of the roof. Everywhere I looked, I saw snow. It was like a blanket to the trees. I started walking toward the steps to go inside. I got the house key under the mat and opened the door. Mom was shocked.

 "Come in, come in! I was so worried! How was the talk with Alexandra?"

"Horrible," I mumbled. I took a deep breath and took off my shoes. They were wet from the snow. I went upstairs to my room and lay down on my bed. I took a minute to process everything that was happening, and I wanted to go to sleep. Eventually, my dull, dark-brown eyes shut down. The cold breeze of the wind flew into my bedroom. It made me feel cold, which helped me sleep. My dreams were black and white, like some people's personalities. I was smiling while sleeping, and I think I know why. Tomorrow's the weekend.

❖ ❖ ❖

I woke up at nine. I stretched and had a smile on my face. I was relaxing in my bed on the best day of the week. Oh, Saturday! You're so peaceful and delightful. I got ready and went downstairs. Mom had already made my egg, and I sat down at the table with her. She was watching a drama on her phone as usual. She loves them, mainly preferring dramas about kings and queens.

I was eating my seasoned egg when Mom turned off her phone. She looked at me, then darted off to the shiny wooden floor.

"Is there something you want to tell me?" I asked.

She took a deep breath.

"Monica, would you like to go to the mall today?"

"I think I can go," I replied.

Mom looked shocked.

"Finally, you're going to go with me? I've been asking you all these years, and you gave me a strong no because you were too busy studying. Are you the true Monica? This isn't a prank, right? What's happening?"

"Mom, relax. I would love to go with you."

She warmly smiled, and I asked Mom what time we would leave. She looked at the clock and told me we could leave at 12. It was nine-thirty at the time, so I decided to read so the time would fly by. I got my book and started reading. Reading relieved me, as if there were no problems in life. It helped me escape from reality. It helped me feel better about myself.

When the clock struck 12, I went with Mom to the mall. I looked outside and saw the snow had melted. I sat in the car, and we left for the mall. I was on my phone, playing a game. Mom was watching the boring gray road with the white signs. Well, obviously. It's not like she was trying to crash the car. I turned off the game and tried to search for references for a new phone case. The one I had was a blue case with blue butterflies on it. It is a typical phone case design, and I want a minimalistic one. It could be a full color. I turned off my phone and decided to look outside. Mom knew I was good with directions, so I tested that. I wanted to see if I could find the name we were driving on. I kept looking at the sides of the road, and we finally came across a traffic light. I looked around the traffic lights for the boring blue sign, and I found it. The road's name was Hanna Valley, although it wasn't a valley. I patted myself on the back and kept looking at the road. I saw that some of the white paint in the middle of the road was fading. Same for the yellow paint.

At the next traffic light, I was looking for the street name and saw a homeless man walking down the stone platform in the middle of the road. He knocked on our stained windows, and I could tell how hard it must've been for him. He had dirt stained on his face, and his hair was as long as five feet! His face had petechiae all over it, and your typical two eyebrows were combined into one unibrow. His lips were grainy and chapped, and he had an elongated beard connected to a mustache. I can't imagine the last time he shaved. He was wearing a brown shirt with holes all over. His shirt had multiple shades of gray. The shirt displayed a white text saying "Love Everyone," even though that has a few exceptions. His pants were these gray sweatpants that people wore to bed. You know when someone wants to relax in bed? They would wear those sweatpants. If you watched television on a couch, you would wear those sweatpants.

Someone who was working at home for the day would wear them. They had holes and brown dirt stains on them as well. So many holes of different sizes made me feel dizzy.

"Uhh, hello, ma'am. I know this is kinda weird to ask, but could you please give me some money?" His voice was vast and deep. Even hearing it startled me a bit. Hearing him ask for money made me feel sympathy. People have no money and are forced to live on the rough, concrete streets. It isn't getting any better with inflation. But thankfully, this man lives in Virginia. It has the inflation-reduction act. It helps reduce energy use and lowers energy costs.

"I'm sorry, but we don't have an-" I cut Mom off.

"C'mon, Mom! We must donate some money to this poor gentleman. He needs it more than we do." I grabbed Mom's high-end purse and admired the brown stars on it. The primary color was beige, so seeing the stars and background contrast was beautiful. I opened it and pushed it to the driver's side to ensure the poor man didn't see any of Mom's personal information. He was on my window side from the passenger seat. Mom's purse is messy, so it was challenging to find her wallet. I looked through her sunglasses, doctor's files, and phone. There were stray papers all around the bag. I eventually found her deluxe black wallet and gave her a severe look.

"Here you go!" I gave him 20 dollars. The smile he had when I gave it to him was something you would give anything to see.

"God bless you little girl." He was surprised and cheerfully left while holding his money up high. I could foresee him as a gentle person. I wonder if he was a father and was asking for money to feed his kids. Maybe he lost his business from the coronavirus. What if he was forced to quit his job? What job could he have had in his business?

When we arrived, I was in awe of the mall. I haven't been there in years, and now I'll see what I've missed out on. It's called Velvet Square, and as far as I know, it has six floors! One is fully dedicated to food. The mall had a gigantic billboard in front of it that advertised a Fashion Elegance store. It is a hit clothing store, and is personally one of my favorites. Although, it has a tremendous problem. The store is so popular that it has gigantic lines! As far as I remember, we couldn't even shop there half the time because of the lines. I hope they fixed them by now.

Mom was trying to find parking, and my jaw dropped. There were a billion cars in the garage. Vehicles colored blue, white, black, and red were all over the space. I saw one dark blue car with a giant scratch on the side.

Mom took five minutes to find a parking spot. It was light years away from the mall. I groaned as we would have to take a tedious walk. We exited the car, and I realized I had forgotten to tie my pink shoes. I tied them and discovered one of the laces was fragmented. As we were at the mall, I didn't mind it. I could ask Mom to buy me some new shoes. I started to walk with her while admiring the pleasing nature. While on the walk, we had to go down these dirty stairs. We went down and had to get past this road to get in. A crossing guard controlled multiple cars lined up, trying to get through. In my opinion, the crossing guard was unnecessary. The vehicle drivers could've just worked it out.

When we went inside the mall, I wondered what store to go into.

"We should look around and find a high-quality store," I said.

Mom knew her directions, but she didn't say anything or use the map, which led us to Fashion Elegance. I patted her on the back, and we entered the pleasing store.

When I walked in, I was stunned. Clothes were

everywhere, and there were so many people. The store had white walls with racks of clothing everywhere. All the colors around me gave me a headache. There were purses, socks, shoes, shirts, and pants. I just came in and already found clothes I loved. And when I looked at the corner of the store, I was shocked. There were multiple floors! How would I search through all of them?

"Oh my god. This is clothing heaven! How about we search through this area first?" My mind was fuzzed with all this. How did I miss this? Did I miss out on other things, too?

"I don't know how I let you miss out on this. Get anything you want, Monica. I have saved so much money for this occasion."

I didn't listen. I was too focused on the clothes. There are so many colors and so many styles. It was like it never ended. After looking for clothes for Mom, we went to the cash register. I was astonished when they were self-checkouts. I missed out on a lot. I still remember the days without the self-checkouts. We had to wait for a long time. I got a plain pink sweatshirt and a few black-and-white shirts and pants. Mom got some blue pants and a yellow shirt. I insisted on her getting more, but she kept telling me she had enough clothes. When we finished checking out, we left the store.

We had a relieving conversation and walked around. I found a Harmonize store and asked Mom if we could go inside. Harmonize is a hydration store. And immediately, she gave me the Mom look. I needed clarification.

"Is this my daughter?" I started laughing, and then she began to laugh. We entered the store, and it smelled like cookies fresh out of the oven. I have never seen so many hydration products in my life. I started to look around the store. There were skin care products, perfume, hand sanitizer, lip care products, and more. I didn't see anything I wanted, but Mom persuaded me to get hand sanitizer for my bag. She wanted me to be able to sanitize my hands whenever I could, and I could understand that. She is germaphobic and constantly wants me to maintain good hygiene. But I would mainly use it for travel, especially in an airport.

Mom wanted some perfume, so I gave her one with her favorite scent and color. It was called Magic Gorgeous and scented with pink strawberries. When I handed it to her, she hugged me. I didn't expect her to like the perfume that much. I got some perfume as well. The one I got was called Everlasting Ocean, which soothed me. It reminded me of sitting on the end of a boardwalk, listening to the sounds of the ocean, and keeping my feet in the cold, salty water. I felt like I was drifting off at sea just by looking at it and smelling the perfume. Once we got all the products we wanted, we did one last stroll around the stop to make sure we had everything we wanted.

We kept looking, and I saw something I could never resist—lip gloss. You can call me a diva all you want, but lip gloss differs from other cosmetics. There were so many choices. It was so hard to choose. There was red, purple, pink, all the good colors. The tubes were so thin. They were as narrow as pencil lead. The fine print was a bubbly font, and the cap was translucent. After some time, I finally chose a radiant pink lip gloss. Mom didn't want any since she had lipstick at home, so we went to the cash register. I was dismayed when I saw the bill.

"61 DOLLARS!?" I loudly whispered in Mom's ear.

"Monica, I told you that you could get anything you want. I have enough money for this." Instantly, she swooped her credit out. I was cranky at her since she spent so much money.

When we left the delightful store, I asked Mom to go home. I didn't want her to spend more money. But Mom begged me to go to another store. I grieved and went with her nagging. While leaving the store, I saw a rest area with fresh plants. There was a podium with three trees on top. All the trees looked newly harvested and fake. It seemed to me that the trees were plastic. So I went and touched one, and I was right. The bark didn't feel rough like a real tree. It felt hard, like plastic. The bark didn't have an accurate color. It was gray.

Mom was walking away, so I left the rest area and ran to her. She was staring at her phone case, and it looked like she wanted to buy a new one. I was shocked, as hers was delightful! Her phone case was just plain pink, but it was so simple. She didn't go too extra. She inspired me, and I wanted a phone case like hers.

"Mom, could we go to a phone case store?" I asked.

"You want a new phone case?" Mom inquired. "I thought you liked the blue with butterflies on top. You used to say you loved it."

"I don't know anymore. It feels old."

"Not today, Monica. We're only getting clothes today. Maybe next time."

That's what she always says. But I went along, and we were walking to our last store. The mall floor had clean tiles despite so many people stepping on them. I thought of the school lunchroom tiles and gagged. There was food everywhere on the floor. I couldn't imagine even touching it! The floor in the lunchroom is extraordinarily dusty and filthy. I noticed that there were plants on every corner. And yes, they were plastic. It was an intelligent decision since watering all those plants would be agony. It would give civilians a dreadful impression if they had dead plants everywhere. I looked at the ceiling, and it shined like the sun. It had a marbled pattern, and a huge chandelier. Imagine being inside a castle. The chandeliers were crafted that way. There were multiple chandeliers, and they would come once every ten stores. There were a few small candelabras, and they helped join the giant one. They had tiny glass droplets, and they formed a circle once together. I couldn't imagine how time-consuming the droplets were to make.

The next store we went to was a clothing store called Misbahzz. When I went in, the store had a cozy-like feel. It mainly consisted of wood, and you would feel like you were in a cottage in the winter. There were colorful clothes all over, each shining with an independent color. I saw many decent clothes to my liking. Mom immediately saw a dress that she liked. It was a white dress with purple roses. The roses looked stylish and realistic. She grabbed it and checked for her size. It was her exact size. It looked like it could fit like a glove. Then she checked every mom's nightmare: the price tag. She looked at it and took a breath of relief. I then started looking for my clothes. Since Mom bought me so many clothes, I decided not to get too much. After 20 minutes, I found a few cute outfits I wanted. I was ready to check out when I saw Connor.

He was checking out his clothes, and I didn't mind it. I kept looking at my clothes when I saw him look oddly discouraged. I was suspicious and saw this white shelf with a feathery texture displaying shoes. I hid behind it, and I could hear them talking clearly.

"I'm sorry, son, but I can't afford these clothes. They're too expensive," Connor's mom murmured.

"As usual," he mumbled.

"I'm sorry, son. I'm trying my best."

I was stunned. Connor only had a few clothes on the counter, and one of them was a pair of socks. Was he poor? I felt sorrow for him. It made me feel ungrateful. Like I took everything I had for granted. I took a deep breath and encouraged myself that it wasn't true. I decided to look for Mom and ask her to check out the clothes I found. I was hoping Connor wouldn't see me, but he took the slightest glance while we were walking out of the store. He did a double take, making sure I was indeed standing there.

"Hey, Monica! What a coincidence I saw you!"

Connor smiled. His disappointed face immediately switched to a grin.

"Oh, hi, Connor," I blandly replied.

"Who's this?" Connor's mom asked.

"Oh, this is my friend Monica," he answered.

"Well, hello! My name is Liana."

"Hello, Liana," I waved at her.

"We have to go, but it was nice meeting you." Liana was a comforting person with a soft voice.

"Goodbye!"

"Goodbye, Liana."

Now I'm keeping a secret from my friend's family. I am the best friend ever.

✧ Chapter Four ✧

The next day, I couldn't believe it. I found such a dirty secret about Connor. I never thought about him being poor. I always assumed he was a rich kid because of the way he acted. That must be where "Don't judge a book by its cover" comes in.

It was Sunday, and Mom and I decided to rest. After breakfast, I rested on my brown armchair and grabbed my favorite book. The armchair had a lever that added an extended legrest, so I pulled it. A folded black blanket was on top of the armchair, so I grabbed it and laid it on my legs. It had a white trellis design. It was so soft. I smiled when I rubbed my hand on the fur.

I was about to finish the book and couldn't stop reading. I loved the cream paper with the book cover. After 10 minutes of reading, I felt like I needed a snack. I was *this close* to finishing, but some chips and reading could hit the spot. Relaxing on such a forsaken chair with all of that would be legendary. I pulled the lever to put the leg rest back and got up. I went to a door that opened to my pantry. The pantry door was a white plywood door. The doorknob was golden, and I could see my reflection on it. I opened the door and grabbed a snack. I walked back to the armchair and sat down. I opened the leg extender and put the blanket on my legs. I got the snack and started eating while reading.

I finished the book five minutes later, so it wasn't worth getting the snack. Eating the snack made me feel like a stress eater. When I finished the book, I shut it hard. I just stood still for a few seconds. The ending was fascinating, and I wish I could have reread the book. The sensational feeling of finishing a project satisfied my standards. I would give anything to reread a good book for the first time. That feeling is worth dying for.

When I snapped back to reality, I walked over to my computer to do some homework. We had to study for a history test, and I would die if I got a score lower than 94 percent. Study, study, study, and my weekend flew by.

    Everywhere around me, I could sense despair. I felt overwhelmed. The next thing I knew, I was waking up and school was starting.

    Before joining everyone at school, I played my cards and tried to remember everything. Cramming information is a monumental weakness of mine. When I want to remember something, I can't. It makes me feel like I have short-term memory loss. When Mom dropped me off outside the school, I kissed her on the cheek and smiled at her. I told her that I loved her and left the car. I didn't want to leave her without saying goodbye, so I waved goodbye and left. She has stories of being less fortunate. For example, when Mom was in elementary school, there were two swings. She would try to come to school as early as possible to go on those swings. A long line of kids would wait to go on one. It was a heartwarming tale. Hearing these stories makes me feel great sympathy for her.

    The word goodbye slipped out of my mouth a little too loud, and everyone heard me. I walked through everyone while the students were giving me weird looks. I chuckled with a dark tone. I put my head down with both hands covering the side of my head. I looked down at the light gray concrete, wanting to stab myself with a knife. The iridescence of the concrete showed my face. Mom was waving to me, and I slightly raised my hand to wave back to her. She quickly drove off, and I took a deep breath. All the kids looked back to see Mom. While everyone was distracted, I rushed inside the school. All the kids turned around, not to find me, and I sighed in relief. I was going to predict the rumors about me. If Vanessa learned about this, her mouth would turn me six feet under. Words are deadly tools if you know how to use them. Even small moments like these can ruin me.

I dodged the crowd and made it to my locker. My locker isn't too shabby. It is a standard high school locker from the movies. It isn't painted pink or blue. It's gray, with three straight rectangular holes on the top. Nobody has ever posted sticky notes outside my locker door. You can open the locker with a four-digit pin. Mine is 2012. It doesn't have those cursed nobs that you have to twist. Those can jam your locker door.

Someone told their best friend their locker pin, and let's just say that it did not end well. Coincidentally, someone had spray-painted curse words all over their locker, and they got into a catastrophic quandary. Do you want to know what people say about coincidences? They don't exist.

I once again noticed the scratches on my locker from past students. I typed in my pin and opened my dull locker. It has a sweatshirt on the third shelf and a water bottle on the top next to a few scrunchies. The scrunchies were very soft, colored light blue, white, and gentle, aesthetic pink. A few had some luxury designs. My notebooks and class textbooks were all on the top two shelves. I don't put anything on the bottom shelf. Who would bend down to grab something from a locker?

I saw my red language arts book and grasped it. It had a paperback cover, unlike most textbooks. The classroom is far from my locker, so I started walking there at a slightly faster pace. I saw Alexandra and gave her a devilish look. She tried approaching me, so I began to fully speedwalk. I turned around and saw her stretching her skinny arm, trying to reach me. I walked through the scattered halls until I arrived just in the corner of the classroom. I was about to open the door to enter the class when I couldn't believe my eyes.

The laugh on their faces and their cunning smiles could make anyone stay away from them. The red liquid on their fists gave me an intense look of aversion. Their ballistic means of pleasure showed me that they're simpletons. Their infuriating means of "being cool" showed their addiction to social media. They're so self-possessed that they think they're better than everyone else.

    I saw Drew and Ester punching and kicking a fragile girl. There was a deep red color of blood on their shoes and hands. Colette was the girl whom Drew and Ester harassed. She had glasses with a dark brown rim. Her skin was ashened. It reminded me of the gray sky. She was holding a blue journal that reminded me of a diary. It looked severely damaged, and I assume that Drew and Ester damaged it. What if Drew and Ester read it? Colette had acne, and she had visible pimples all over her face. She was short and stubby, like a gnome. One of those garden gnomes your neighbor has describes her accurately. Her hair had knots all over it.

    How does it feel to be treated that way? How does it feel to have your young, warm blood wasted by some other humans? How does it feel to be beaten down and have nothing to do about it? How does it feel to be less fortunate than others? How does it feel to be in her shoes? I watched in despair, with all these questions popping into my mind. I could feel my body sinking. And then, I couldn't control myself. I just started moving when I didn't want to. I didn't want to help her. I wanted to stay in my cocoon, in my shell. I didn't want to get into this. Why did I help her? Did I do the right thing?

I stepped up, standing in the position of a star. I stood in front of Colette.

"Hey! Don't touch her." I gave them an evil look until I finally came to my senses. What am I doing? Why am I helping her? I eyed her; it was a staring contest. I wrinkled my right eye at Ester, threatening her. It was like being in the lower class and threatening someone in the high class.

Suddenly, Ester grabbed me by my arms. She had a firm grip, and I couldn't wiggle out.

"Let's hurt both of them," Ester announced. She nudged me next to Colette, and Drew was about to lay a punch. I braced myself, hoping to be saved by a miracle. He moved his arm and curled his hands for the final blow, and soon, he hit me.

It felt like his fist was sinking into my stomach. It was like I couldn't breathe. My lungs had disappeared, abandoning me. I was going to throw up. Nobody was watching, so nobody saw how I looked. Everyone was in class. I ran away from them and just opened the door to class. I was limping, and Mrs. Hamlet saw me.

"You're late to class. Why are you limping?" She wondered.

"I hit my leg. I need a few minutes to recover. Don't worry, I'm fine." Lying is the only thing I'm good at. I walked to my desk and took out my books. I looked around at other students who stared at me. I looked down at the tiled floor that reflected a face of embarrassment. It bounced off the walls and transmitted to everyone. Two incidents in one day!? I'm not being careful. I put my hand on my stomach, and my arm held my sadness. It felt worse than a movie spoiler when you dreamed of watching that movie for years.

After class, I walked out, and upon me was Colette. I took a deep breath, not wanting to look at her. I curled my fist with a reminder about what happened. Her face showed it all. I walked to my next class, and Colette chased me. She put her index finger up, showing her desire to speak. I started to walk faster, which eventually turned into a speedwalk.

"T-thank you for h-helping me." She stuttered commonly, which advised me that she could be an introvert. I wouldn't be surprised if she has social anxiety.

I looked down at my white, bitten nails and everyone else's overdone nails. I felt like I was ignoring her, but if I defended her, it would make no sense to blank her.

"Hmm," I groaned.

"Most people wouldn't do something like that." She smiled and winked. And she is right.

Everyone stands back when the bullying happens. But I didn't stand back. I was one of the valiant kids who fought back. Her saying that made me feel proud. Like I was vital and different.

I was finally a hero.

My expression changed when she said that. Her words soothed me. I looked at her as if I had never heard those words before. I winced my eyes and thought about being courageous and that I was.

"Thank you," I muttered.

"Would you like to be friends?"

I thought for a moment. If I became friends with her, it could affect me. Although, it would warm her heart if we were together. How many friends does she have in the first place?

"I'll think about it." I should've said yes. That response was stupid.

I walked to my locker with her. She was heartwarming, and I thought she was unique. I opened my locker and checked the alarm clock inside it. I looked at the time and squinted my eyes. It was 8:55, and history starts at nine! I have my test! I snagged my book and began to run over to the classroom. I don't want the history teacher, Mrs. Trapini, to count points off because I was late! She's strict when it comes to arriving on time. She will still count you late if you come seconds after the bell rings. Seconds!

I opened the door to the classroom, and I was well acquainted with a frosty breeze. Mrs. Trapini's classroom was always chilly, and everyone wore sweatshirts. I shivered and walked over to my desk. I checked the clock, and it showed 8:59, so I blew off a sweat. I looked at my dirty pink sneakers and was shaking when the bell rang. I flicked my nails until Mrs. Trapini finally decided to give the test. I looked over her hands, grasping the test papers, and thought of Mom with her doctor's notes. Mrs. Trapini walked around the classroom, passing out the test packets. She came to me, gave me my test, and I picked out my lucky black pencil. Coincidentally, it says good luck on it. The text was gold, making me feel rich. I looked around to see everyone using their pencils on paper. I took a deep breath and started the test. I could feel water dripping down my face. My hands were sweating. I turned around to be awaited by the clear, transparent window. I heard the wind and the trees rustle. The grass faced the direction of the wind. I stood up straight and finally started the test.

It was a 40-question test with one question I hate. Question 19: my lifelong affliction. "Who was the first explorer to sail around the world?" Okay, I made the stupid mistake of choosing Christopher Columbus instead of Ferdinand Magellan. I'm sorry, okay? I missed some bright notes and forgot to study that insipid part. I thought that question was simple, but I must've overlooked that questions are never *that* simple. And before you try to correct me with two plus two, think about how you *really* solve it. Yeah, you add two plus two, and you get four! Simple! Right? Right? Riiiiight?

You're correct.

Next time you do two plus two, think about the process of the problem. How do you get from two to four?

I'm weird.

The essence of worried students uttered, and I predicted when the ball would ring. It was a count of three, and the infamous bell rang. I immediately got my book and ran out of the door. I took a deep breath and slowly walked to my locker. I could hear all the students talking, their scarce breath coming into my ears. I pinched the locker pin and typed one-nine-eight-zero. I stared at my blank white nails that were supposed to be pink. I bit them as well.

When I was home, I felt guilty. Today wasn't a good day at school. Of course, Mom wasn't home, so I went upstairs and wanted to rest.

I lay on my bed, feeling depressed. I wasn't in the mood for anything today.

A few tears came into my eyes.

Life sucks, doesn't it? The immense pressure to do well in everything, the fear of encountering bullies, isn't it overwhelming? I wonder what Grandpa would think about me. I miss him. He believed in me for everything and encouraged me to study. He had such a good soul.

He didn't deserve his fate.

Flashback

I walked with him to the kitchen to make cookies. I was happily holding my grandpa's warm, wrinkly hand. I smiled and stared at his hairy chin, looking at his wise mustache. Grandpa was a wise man. Without him, I wouldn't be the person I am today. He inspired me to work hard for his approval. He had white hair and skin. I strived to be like him and always worked hard on all my assignments. I never stopped thinking about how proud he would be if I showed him assignments with flawless grades. With that wholesome smile and glint in his eye, I would die to see his proud face.

One thing about him that I always loved was how wise he looked. You could tell he was clever with the way he acted. Grandpa always wore glasses with a black rim, especially when reading a book. And it reminded me of a political man. Grandpa was very political, especially in American politics. I don't want to get into politics. They make me feel awkward. I know how people don't always agree with them. People have lost everything due to politics. Do you know about words? Words are powerful if you can use them correctly. Their incorrect use is what causes wars.

You wouldn't ever find someone with his personality on the web. He looked unique in a delicate and prestigious way. He always had the best quality. He knew what to buy and what wasn't worth our time. He was an astounding cook despite his age. Maybe a better cook than Mom. Let me tell you, those words are shocking coming from me.

In the kitchen, I grabbed the shiny mixer. Grandpa corralled the chocolate chips. I had a major obsession with chocolate chips. My grandpa put his index finger up and pointed at me. He told me not to eat any. Grandpa would never pique at me. I creased my black, messy eyebrows with confusion. He opened his chapped lips from his mouth and sent me to grab butter, flour, eggs, and brown sugar. My whole family never liked white sugar. We always used brown sugar. I still don't know why they preferred it. I assume it was because it's thicker, but I don't know much about sugar.

I looked around the cluttered pantry and rolled my eyes. Mom has the messiest pantry. She constantly reminded me to care for my room and desk. But I would never listen, and as a cherry on top, I would remind her about this area, and she would stop talking. You name it: snacks, seasoning, containers with flour and sugar, it has everything. It was mesmerizing for my tiny dark-brown eyes to see all the snacks. I widened my eyes, desperately searching for the ingredients. I didn't want to be late for him. I looked around the pantry until I found everything. I ran to Grandpa and stood beside him, giving him all the ingredients. He warmly smiled at me when I gave him the ingredients, and I stood there feeling like a hero. I waited for him to finish adding all the ingredients, flicking my nails on the way. He told me to separate the wet and dry ingredients, and I nodded while making duck lips.

I commonly made cake with Mom at home (at that time), and she taught me about keeping ingredients separate. I looked at Grandpa's happiness while adding the batter, mixing, and having fun. Cookies were my favorite dessert, even with my sweet tooth. I had a giant sweet tooth when I was little. I mean giant.

After every single meal, I would eat something sweet. I tried to contain it, but no matter what I tried, I couldn't. The shocking part was that Mom never warned me to stop. I had to learn by myself to stop. Mom always bought me sweets and never told me to stop eating them. I still wonder why she never warned me but wanted me to learn independently. Mom would buy it if I told her I didn't want to eat it. If I told her I wanted it badly, knowing I couldn't eat it, she would tell me it was okay.

You can eat it.

Those words still pain me today. Knowing I could've had such a horrible addiction. I could've ended up with, like, a disease or something.

I watched the counter, thinking the black spots on the glazed granite could move. I hallucinated a lot back then. I was stuck in a trance until Grandpa patted my shoulder. I looked around in worry, quickly gasping when I saw him. My problems with trances were horrible, and whenever I was doing my work, focused, I would look at something and forget what I was doing. I gave him a look with a silly glare. Everyone in the family always laughed at my witless faces. Grandpa laughed as well, and he made me laugh. I looked up to Grandpa's tall body to see him loudly chuckling. I pretended to giggle, not understanding the joke. He stopped laughing, and I closed my mouth. We went on to make the cookies.

It was only a few minutes later when he fainted.

Don't worry; he didn't die yet. But a few weeks later, a gruesome trip to the hospital marked him six feet under.

I still wonder to this day if I was the cause of his death. But don't worry. Mom calmed me down by telling me that his death could happen at any moment.

She said a graceful daughter like me would never

cause something so cruel.
Like I am so graceful.

✧ Chapter Five ✧

I am going to get back at Alexandra and her friends. I will need Connor's help, but he can't be the only one who will help me.

I have to get her.

I have "history" with my friends. Old friends, I should say. But I have to get back to the start of high school, where it all began. I moved from California, worried about my first day of school. Mom was confident I would be the most fabulous girl ever! She was a prominent person for my confidence. When I walked into that school, I was trembling. My worry was visible to the aliens in a parallel universe. I was friendless and lonely at the start of the year. Nobody wanted to be with me.

They called me the "weird nerdy girl."

But then I became friends with them. We were all the "weird kids." The ones who were never in drama. The ones that only thought of each other as funny. (Nobody, and I mean nobody, thought we were funny). But we were perfect together, and we had no insecurities. We were confident. We didn't care about people's comments about us.

Then came the sophomore year, where they were mean to me. On top of that, I was stressed because of all the tests and couldn't take them. They always said mean phrases and called me an idiot for no reason. They were all I had back then.

In the second quarter, they decided to stop being friends with me. After that, I never went to recess. I always stayed inside and worked on assignments. I don't know why they stopped being friends with me. At the very end of the school year, they forgave me. Boom, we were friends again, and everything was okay. Right?

Now, junior year, or the year I'm currently in. I was so excited to see them on the first day of school. I was so innocent back then. I still trusted them. Looking back, I was too soft. I needed to get back to reality instead of being a marshmallow. Well, we all know how that turned out. But I'm going to get back at them. And trust me, they're going to regret it.

I'll need Connor's help. After helping him with math, he owes me. Besides, he would do anything for me. Connor knows about popularity. I can't just get them back. I need to rise against them.

I need to prove that I'm better than them.

There's only one person that will do the trick.

The one and only.

The one who was the most popular for one year. The one who knows every trick in the book for popularity. The key. She knows the rules for dressing. She knows the key to style. She knows the rules, what to do, how to be beautiful. She will be the one who will help me insert my dominance.

Violet.

The old queen bee.

So when I went to school the next day, I knew I had to plead to her for help. When I arrived at school, I felt troubled. I didn't want to talk to her. I felt like she would call me a nerd. That is Violet's personality in a nutshell, after all. I walked through the rotted school gates feeling like the odd one out. Everyone there had friends, but I was stuck in the corner. I looked around to see the usual. Everyone was standing in their area of the halls. I walked through everyone until I saw her. Her appearance was staggering.

Her looks didn't change at all. Violet had short, silky black hair like me. She had a dark tan skin color. Violet is very short, five feet at most. She always wore a crop top with shorts. Her shorts were decently long. I wasn't surprised to see her wear a pink vertical-striped top. She typically wears it. Her shorts were short black jeans with a few rips. Why are ripped jeans even "trendy?" You have lovely jeans, and you ruin them. What is the point?

Her legs had a few minor bruises and scratches. I wouldn't be surprised if they were from the soccer games she played with her friend. She wore one bracelet on her left arm (her dominant arm) and two bracelets on her right arm. I love to tease her about being a lefty. I looked down and saw her wearing one anklet. It had a shiny golden chain with crystal butterfly charms. I knew butterflies meant positive change, and they reminded me of my lock-and-key earrings. I thought about my earrings and thought about their symbolism.

"Hey, Violet! So, I need to inform you about something."

"Yeah? What is it?"

"So," I paused for a moment. "I kinda, maybe, sorta lost all my friends."

"WHAT!?" She shouted so loud everyone in the hallway heard. We were getting weird stares from everyone. "How?"

"It's a long story," I told her everything because I know you don't want to reread the whole story. It took me so long to retell it.

The first bell rang right when I finished. It scared the life out of us. Then we started to guffaw together. Isn't that the talent of school bells?

"I'm going to class. We'll have a big talk about this. A *big* talk." She gave me a glance that told me I should be scared. I laughed and walked to language arts.

I wondered if I was doing all these things wrong. Holding my book, I stared at it, thinking about everything I'd ever read in a book. They're a whole new world. I clutched it tightly, regaining my focus and walking toward the classroom, remembering how books are part of my life. The nostalgia made me break into a chuckle. I knew I would never be alone because I would always have a book.

Language arts was boring. I'm already the best writer in the class. Why do I need to stay in the lecture? When I was eleven, I wrote and read at the ninth-grade level. At that age, I constantly studied writing. I had one goal: to publish a book.

My journey started with pure, dazzling boredom. That was my whole motivation. Without it, I wouldn't be the queen of writing I am today, and I wouldn't have been constantly determined to improve my writing.

My first attempt at a decent book was called "Happy..?" It was about a girl named Hester who got kidnapped when she was little. She trained to be an assassin in a group called Ash. I still have the manuscript and cringe in disgust when I stare at it. The writing is like a first grader. First of all, it used a weird serif font that nobody uses. I liked a different serif font better, even before I started writing my book. So why did I use that weird font? I don't know to this day. I didn't align my text, either. The left side was straight like a ruler, but the right was a mess. And the font size, oh, I won't even talk about that. It was fifteen! The recommended font size for a book was twelve! The headings were size thirty. T-h-i-r-t-y.

You probably have no idea about what I am ranting about. You notice your mistakes from your second draft to your first. Speaking about the second draft, that's where I'm going to move on. My second draft was called "A Black Broken Eye." It was about a girl named

Courtney who had bibliophilia, a love for books. But she took this too far. No, she didn't have a black, broken eye. She didn't have any friends, and all she did was read. She would often hallucinate, confusing reality with characters from her books. A Black Broken Eye was the book I went far with. It made it to 47 pages but stopped due to high school.

I started it in fifth grade and dreamed of self-publishing it.

I told you there was one reason I started writing books. But I lied. There are two.

It would be best if you braced yourself for the second reason.

I did it for popularity. In fifth grade, I felt terrible that I wasn't as cool as all the other girls. The situation is the same for sixth grade. I was shy, and all I wanted to do was become popular. I had a friend named Astrid. She was the most fantastic girl ever! She had long brown hair and was excruciatingly tall. She was so lovely but wasn't the most wise. She wasn't wholly dumb like other kids but wasn't the brightest either. She had forced Asian parents, and I always noticed her sadness every day. I tried to make her feel better, but she promised me she was okay. The valid golden rule is when someone says they're fine, they aren't fine. It's called having empathy.

All I wanted was to be like her. Everyone loved her. I tried everything, from changing my personality to changing my style. But all my effort didn't do a thing. But I don't care about that now. All that matters is being on the podium.

At lunch, I met up with Violet to talk to her. She needs to fix me, apparently. Once I walked in, I was again met with the dirty breeze of lunch food. I desperately searched for her table and happily skipped to it once I saw it. I scooched against all the students, apologizing every time I passed someone. Violet saw me while I skipped, and I gave her a shy wave. She waved back while responding with a witty face. I grinned and gave her a long stare. I should have looked around my surroundings because I bumped into Vanessa.

Except I didn't just bump into her.

I spilled her orange juice all over her.

"Oh my god! I'm so sorry! Do you need help?" I rushed over to a nearby table and grabbed tons of napkins. I ran back to her and handed her all of them in a panicked manner. "It was an accident! I'm sorry. Please forgive me. I promise I won't do it again!" She was so mad. She clenched her fists like she was about to punch me.

"Urgh!" She stomped away and shouted at someone to move when they were in front of her. Why am I such a screw-up?

After the incident, I shamefully walked over to Violet's table. My head was down, and I slouched my shoulders. Somehow, I had a peculiar feeling inside of me. I felt worried that she was going to do something to me. My heart was pumping, and I started to get a toothache. I used a technique I learned to try to calm myself down.

I joined my hands, slowly closed my eyes, and imagined I was eating chocolate cake.

Did you think it was an exciting ritual a witch named Blair would do? This isn't fantasy. I think. Sitting at Violet's table, I expected her to lecture me on how ludicrous I was, how I screwed everything up, and how I could never do anything right.

I looked at her. She face-palmed herself when she knew I was watching her.

"You're dead. That girl is the queen of the school. She will destroy you just like you destroyed her designer bag. You should prepare for the storm. Do you need me to give you lessons? I could teach you the basics of school logic," her sarcasm is amusing.

"I think I already know what school is, thank you

very much. You're treating me like a new girl who was homeschooled."

"Well, you act like one."

I was offended by that comment. I scoffed and turned around to talk to Violet's best friend, Ria. Let me tell you, she is as fast as Usain Bolt! She plays soccer six out of seven days a week. She is short but the opposite of stubby. She has short brown hair, and Violet always encourages her to wear her hair down. She doesn't like it down, which is similar to my preference. Ria had a million freckles between her nose and eyes and was so, so stubborn. Her most lively trait is how energetic she acts. All her soccer does good for her. Here's the shocking part: she's vegetarian. Not vegan. There is a difference. Vegans don't eat dairy. Her excuse is she doesn't want to kill animals, but she doesn't mind taking from them. She has two sisters, Erica and Carmin. I can't tell a single difference between their faces. Erica is older than Ria and looks exactly like an older version of her. Carmen is younger than Ria, and I can see her as a younger version of her. Ria's face never changes. She looks the same as she looked in middle school.

I don't want a sister. If I get one, then I won't inherit Mom's riches when she is at age.

By "at age," I mean when she is in her midlife crisis.

Besides, everyone complains about sisters. Sisters wear your clothes, steal your money, and tell lies to get you in trouble.

I went to talk to Ria, and she was surprised I was sitting there. She winced, rubbed her eyes, and finally spoke words when she realized I was sitting here and it wasn't a dream.

"What are you doing here?"

"Hi!" A second later, I softly chortled. Just as I was about to say something, the bell rang. And I loudly respired, learning I hadn't accomplished anything.

When I went home, I saw Mom making food in the kitchen. I wonder what she's making today. I dropped my school bag next to the rusted washer, which reminded me of a memory. One time, the washer randomly exploded, and my school bag smelled like dish soap for days. It was scary. I panicked in case my papers got wet. I had important documents in there, including a few pages of A Black Broken Eye written. The first thing I did was get those papers out. I felt that those papers mattered the most. I thankfully hugged the papers, grateful that they were saved.

Good circumstances only come to you if you think about them. Yes, it is the same for bad ones. And back then, I was very negative.

I walked inside and had the best lunch ever. You know what it is, duck confit.

I went to the table and dug in. I did a small dance while eating it, enjoying it. When I finished, I started doing homework. I couldn't stop thinking about Violet, and I almost jumped when I remembered her old book. We were writing buddies, and I used to help her write her book. However, I became too focused on my book and forgot to help her. Slowly but surely, I stopped working with her entirely.

I wanted to see how her book was doing, so I went to check on it. I ran to my computer and opened my writing software. I was hoping the document was shared with me. I searched it up on the search bar and found it. It showed her name in a serif font, Violet Mercado. I still remember the capital V with pink around it. I remembered how I had a purple smiley face as my profile picture. I opened it, puckered my eyebrows, and rubbed my eyes, wondering if my eyes were deceiving me.

She was writing in the document.

My mouse hovered over the scroll bar, and I went all the way down. It was page 109. I felt nostalgia hit me as I watched her type, "The End." A few seconds passed, and I felt a tear on my cheek. I wish I had the potential to accomplish this strong feat. I took a few deep breaths and interlocked my fingers. I smiled and started to tear up. Ultimately, I was proud of how my friend accomplished my goal. I want to buy her a gift. She deserves to be congratulated.

✧ Chapter Six ✧

"Hey, Mom, could we go to the store? I want to buy my friend a present." I smiled, hoping to convince her to help me with my kindness.

She initially looked skeptical but was convinced when I added this in.

"I'll buy the gift with my own money!" I sang in a funny tone, with the clarity that told her I wouldn't lie. Mom is kind. She will probably let me go.

"Will we go somewhere close by?"

"Of course!"

"Eh, I'm convinced. I have 30 minutes to spare. Where do you want to go?"

"We could go to Killerr Jewels?"

"What store is that?" She asked.

"My friend loves that store. We can search for the directions on your phone. She told me that it is close to our area."

"Sure! Let's go." I went to the smelly shoe rack to put on my pink sneakers. I looked at the shoe size, remembering how I'd been size seven for years. Mom explained that she needed to change her clothes if I wanted to go. I sat on the wrecked dining chair and started to put on my shoes. I imagined Mom telling me she would buy new ones. The black leather had been chipped excessively. There were six chairs, but now there are five. A few months prior, a chair broke. As Mom walked up the stairs, the feeling of revenge took me over. I was so mad at my old friends. I wanted to throw something! I couldn't care about my past. I had to go to the present.

You know, a little bit of revenge wouldn't hurt.

When Mom came downstairs, I pulled down my jacket and went outside to the car. The garage is so dirty. You could not imagine. There is dust and spider webs everywhere. I saw a bug or two in there. Mom's car is even worse. She got it washed by a professional a few days ago. It looked so clean that time. It was a once-in-a-lifetime sight. Immediately the next day, Mom wrecked it. Her doctor's notes, bag, and gifts ruined the car. Her car is a catfish, in a way. Every, and I mean every time I go in that car, I have to move papers and her stethoscope from the passenger seat. Today was not any different. Why would it be? Scooting papers from a seat is my only use to her.

I sat in the uncomfortable seat, shivering. I'm not too fond of it when it's cold—it is February in the Northern Hemisphere—but I hope winter will end soon. When Mom entered the car, just as she was about to start driving, I asked her if she could turn on the seat warmer, the most heavenly feature of a vehicle. It warms you from head to toe! It makes you stop shivering in seconds. Honestly, there are two things every car should have. One: Advanced airbags. Two: An advanced seat warmer. Like the ones in those expensive cars.

When she turned it on, she turned her car keys to start driving.

Our area has so much traffic. If we went there without traffic, arriving would take us thirty seconds. But with our bothersome traffic, it takes five to ten minutes. I know it looks like I'm yapping about nothing, but the traffic can annoy you to the extreme.

I glanced outside to find a herd of deer running. The deer are the worst. So many car crashes have happened because of them. Mom even had a car crash once.

Here's how it happened to Mom. Imagine you are driving on two lanes. You're about to go home, but suddenly, a deer jumped in front of your car! You're supposed to break, right? Well, that's what she did.

And yet she killed the deer anyway. The deer must have been too close to the car. Mom was driving by herself, and I was at home doing homework. I don't have the exact details of the incident. I was so worried that something had happened to her. It was such a scary event! Sometimes, I wonder if you are supposed to keep driving instead of using the break. Wouldn't it encourage the deer to run away from the road, or else it would die? These thoughts clamored my mind. By the time I was about to say a word to Mom, we already arrived. I stepped out of the car, feeling cold again. I groaned and entered the shop.

It is cleaner than I expected. I have never entered this store, but Violet always assured me that it is the best jewelry store. She has begged me for a long time to buy from here. I looked around, with the store having such clean tiles where I could see my face. I furrowed my eyebrows at my reflection and whisked a tiny piece of food off my face. I winked, making the peace sign with my hands, and turned around to look at the store. A piece of jewelry caught my eye, so I trotted to it. The jewelry was very fancy, like some at a designer store. I arrived at the stall and almost wanted to open the glass box to take the ring. It was a snake that wrapped around your finger. I had never seen a ring like it, so I strutted to Mom to ask her to buy the ring. I reminded myself to stay on task. I was supposed to buy something for my friend, not myself.

I wanted to find something for my friend, and I'd return to the ring later. I wanted to buy her a necklace since they are more memorable—just one tiny problem.

I have no idea what to buy her.

I don't want to waste my time trying to find something just for it to be weird. I'm still determining the most memorable symbols. I could ask the shopkeeper what the best symbols are.

So, my adventure began. I went to look for the shopkeeper, wondering what he looked like. Is this store worldwide, or is it only known to be here? Is it a small business? Small businesses have the best quality materials, but they're expensive. Imagine buying some sweatpants for, what, 50 dollars? That does not even include shipping! Most small businesses have those prices. Large companies are cheap but are worse in quality. In a way, I hope this store consists of both qualities—the quality of a small business, but cheap like a large business.

I kept searching but failed. It took me a moment to find the shopkeeper. He was at the bracelet section, showing Mom a diamond bracelet. I approached him, about to ask him about a necklace. I was about to speak, but my sight had to go to the bracelet. The bracelet had these tiny charms, but I couldn't determine what they were. They looked like diamonds. The middle had a small black dot, and the outside was white. I immediately returned to my senses and decided to talk to the keeper.

"Hello, uhh," I read his nametag. "Rob. Could you help me find a necklace for my friend? She finished writing her book, so I want to congratulate her."

"Sure! A necklace, you say?"

"Yep."

He took me to the necklace section. I was shocked at the amount of necklaces. There were at least four stands of necklaces, each holding unique colors, styles, and charms. Each hook was fully stocked.

"Do you want a gold or silver chain for your

friend?"

"Gold, please."

Violet is a huge fan of gold. She doesn't like silver that much.

"Alright. Would you like your friend to have a necklace with random charms or one with a birthstone?"

The one with the birthstone would represent her. One with random charms wouldn't define anything about her. It wouldn't show my appreciation for her.

"I think the birthstone is okay. My friend was born in February."

"Got it! I have an ideal necklace for her."

While he was helping me, I noticed Mom staring at that same bracelet. She has been looking at it for a while. He scurried to this particular section, displaying necklaces with these pigmented jewels. I started to get excited staring at them. They were so pretty!

"Is this okay?" He handed me a beautiful necklace.

Gems surrounded the central purple gem, giving it a rich and defined style. The purple gem shined brightly in the sunlight like it was born for it. It was amethyst, which is one of my favorite gems. (Amethyst is the birthstone for February.) I could already imagine her style and her confidence with the necklace. The amethyst gem was like the main character, and the mini diamond stones were the side characters. I took it from his hands and urgently tried to find Mom.

"Thank you! This necklace is perfect." I bowed to him and walked away. Why would I bow to him? That was weird.

I found Mom in the same section, still staring at the same bracelet. I showed her the necklace, silently begging her to get it. She nodded in appreciation and asked me if there was something I wanted. I eagerly dragged her to the stand with the snake ring, and she could tell I liked it. I put my hands together and kept asking her. Eventually, she gave in. She agreed to buy it. Well, I still had to buy it with my own money. Meh, it's fine. There was something I still wondered. Why was Mom staring at that bracelet? I'm going to ask her.

"Mom, if you don't mind me asking, why were you staring at the bracelet for such a long time?"

"Oh, Monica, I am shocked. Your grandmother had this exact bracelet. I am curious to know how it was here."

After checkout, she thanked the employee, and I stood there in complete confusion.

✧ ✧ ✧

The school was crowded, as usual. But I went in there with one mission: to find Violet. I started to examine the halls, but it was too crowded to see her. I then realized she had to be in one place: the bathroom. Everyone goes in there to do their hair and have an hour-long girl talk. People also do skincare there, thinking they must look perfect for every occasion. In my opinion, wearing makeup to school is a waste of product. You should wear makeup to essential events like parties and weddings. The product finishes in the snap of your fingers. Violet used to try to drag me into makeup, but I never got the gist of it.

 I never realized how many people feel like they're imperfect.

 They don't know the secret of life. Nobody will mention your insecurities if you don't talk about them. Well, they do probably notice your insecurities, but they won't talk about them! If you don't know what people think about you then you should be okay. As long as you are confident with how you look, then that's all that matters. Besides, it's not like people will gossip about you! Right?

 I pushed everyone else away and walked to the bathroom, and I could tell I was close when I smelled the gruesome scent of urine. Some girls stood at the door, so I kneeled and slid past them. I plugged my nose once I came in. I could see Violet's backpack outside the bathroom, so I looked around and found her in the very corner, looking into her eyes. She was trying to pop a pimple with her sharp nails plucking it. I patted her on the shoulder, and she jumped in utter shock.

"Did you see me finish my book? I saw you on the document," she questioned. I could tell she weirdly felt some guilt. The glint in her eye was a sign of fear or distress.

"Yes, and I wanted to congratulate you."

I handed her the necklace, and her smile beamed through everyone.

"W-wow! Thank you, Monica!" She hugged me while holding the necklace. I felt the pride of making someone's day.

I was about to leave for class, but guess who came in?

Vanessa. Oh, her evil smirk would make anybody want to run away. You want to punch her when you see her attractive cheekbones and symmetrical face shape.

Wait a minute, am I complimenting her?

I want to rip my ears off when I hear her voice. I want to pull my hair when I see her acting so fake. At least I'm not entirely made of plastic. I want to go six feet under when I'm trying to hide the fact I'm envious of her. I want to destroy her heart. I want her attractiveness to disappear. I want to destroy everything about her.

She acted like she was the queen of the world. She had a stain on her hand, so she swished her hand in an aspect that got her friend to clean it up for her. How pathetic. She acted like a model and aggressively put her arms down when she saw the necklace in its fancy box. She clenched her fists and did some duck lips as she slowly approached me with a fancy attitude. She put one arm on her side. I don't have a good feeling about this.

"What's this I see?" She snatched the necklace from Violet's hand. She looked like a baby who wanted to play with a toy. She looked at the necklace for a minute, admiring its beauty with the minimalistic diamonds. She looked confused by its beauty. Her face was a little funny. I almost chucked from it.

"This is mine now."

"What, no, this is her property! You can't just take her necklace!"

"Why can't I? Can I get arrested for this?" She did a vengeful chuckle. And she held the necklace behind her shoulders like a model was posing in a picture.

"No, you aren't taking this." I pranced on her, trying to grab the necklace. But I was too short, so she held it high, and I couldn't take it. She laughed like a villain, and I eventually gave up. Violet couldn't get it either. She's shorter than me. I tried to take it back, but she kept dodging my attacks. When she left the bathroom, I was fuming.

Violet looked furious. I decided to take her outside of the restroom. We could talk about this later. There were a lot of girls in the bathroom. Besides, this was a personal problem. I lightly held her shoulders and dragged her out of the bathroom. We walked next to the water fountain. Nobody would hear us talking, and even if they did hear, they wouldn't care. I'm sure of it.

"How could this happen!? Ugh, that idiot! Why can't she go to hell already?"

Violet was silent. I could hear her deep breaths from a mile away. She was dismayed and angry, wanting to leave the world.

"Violet? Are you okay?"

My voice was trembling.

"This ... this means war."

Part Two

Her Whispers

✧ Chapter Seven ✧

"Are you saying we're fighting against her? How, when, now?" It was apparent how confused I was. What do we do? Isn't this risky?

"Of course! When should we attack?" She sounded so serious and confident.

"Violet, are you okay? Are you sure you want to do this? I could buy you another one."

Great. We wasted our money.

"And ruin this chance? She stole our necklace, gossiped about all the students, and acted utterly innocent. I'm done with her. You know what? We have to make a plan."

"A plan? You know what, that isn't that bad of an idea." I tilted my head up, thinking about it. The bell rang, so we had to go to class. I waved goodbye to Violet and started to walk to language arts in utter anguish, ticked off about what had happened.

While walking, Connor came beside me. He looked curious, like he was wondering what happened. I didn't want to tell Connor yet. I don't know if he has entirely changed from his past. Besides, what if he spilled the tea in front of the entire school? I can't trust him yet. I need to know him on a higher level for me to trust him. I need to be as brief about it as possible. Don't spill any tea. Keep most of it secret. Come on, Monica, you can do this!

"Hey, Monica!" He was in a bright and cheerful mood. "How are you doing? Is your life going well?"

"Heh, yeah, super well." I gave a thumbs-up with a fake smile. I hope he couldn't tell that I was lying. I am not the best liar.

"Great! I have to go to science, see you in math!" I let out a sigh of relief. It was a little stupid of me to have that tone when he asked me that question. I guess it's just in my personality to do that.

When I entered the depressing essence of the language arts classroom, I didn't feel like paying too much attention. Then I had a brilliant idea. So I got my language arts notebook on the top of my pile of books and opened it. The smell of old books filled the air. I got my favorite pen and started to write ideas for revenge. It would be a brisk idea to tell Violet.

Ways to Get Revenge

1. Secretly spill something on her in front of the school?
2. Put itching powder somewhere on her body. Maybe in her hair?
3. Embarrass her. Expose her true identity in front of the school.
4. KILL HER!! BURY HER SIX FEET UNDER WHERE SHE DESERVES!
5. Should we become friends with her to stab her in the back?
6. Add permanent paint to her car, saying Monica is the best or something. Yes, I know what her car looks like. It is a vibrant hot pink.
7. Be a witch to her like she is a witch to us.

It was only a short time until class ended. I am an expert at hiding things, possibly because Mrs. Hamlet expects nothing terrible from me, so she does not bat an eye. I closed the notebook in a hostile manner to ensure that nobody could read anything. What if someone stood up and read my writing while leaving class? There are a countless number of students who read people's work without permission. They will approach you, tilt their head, and read your work. The worst part is that they would give criticism. We didn't ask for your opinion. That can't happen with something this risky. Someone can snitch or tell Vanessa. The possibilities are endless!

Connor approached me again. He seemed to be joyful today. But surprisingly, the entire walk was silent—well, almost the whole walk.

I am an empathetic person. I have a "special ability" to tell if people are happy or sad. Due to the internet, a high schooler isn't expected to possess empathy. Social media has destroyed everyone's attention span and logic. But I am not super addicted to social media like everyone else. I do other things with my time, like reading. Since my empathy hasn't drastically lowered, I have a "superpower" in telling people emotions. And Connor looked down. His head was staring at the dirty floor, and he seemed genuinely depressed. It wasn't even two seconds before I decided to speak to him.

"Hey, Con! Can I call you that? Are you okay? Do you need some cheering up? You were so joyful minutes ago!" I asked in a snarky tone. I punched his arm lightly to signal that he was okay.

"Oh, yeah. I just, uhh, might have gotten a bad score on the science test today."

"Really? Well, how bad can it be? You probably got, like, what? 89?"

"First of all, 89 is a great score!"

"Sure," I mumbled.

"You got some standards. I got 67."

"WHAT!?" It jumped out of my mouth. "Oh my god, I'm so sorry." I covered my mouth immediately.

"You're fine. That's how everyone else reacted."

"You're okay, buddy. Everybody messes up. You know, if you got 67, then I'll probably get 55! You're smart, alright? Nobody is perfect, not even the gifted students." I patted him on the back, and he smiled at me. I could tell he felt better already. I was about to walk away, but suddenly, he just hugged me! Butterflies were in my stomach. I felt a new feeling I'd never felt before. It was hearing that someone was truly proud of me. Don't worry, it isn't romantic at all. Blech, romance is disgusting. I decided to let it go and think about it later.

This means that we are getting closer.

The bell rang again, as I had to attend my next class, history. Luckily, Violet is with me in this class. I could show her my plans. However, I wasn't excited to see Mrs. Trapini. She uses her phone while talking to someone, always ignoring you for another student. It's irritating and makes you feel discouraged.

I started to shiver, remembering my primary goal was to find Violet. I was freezing, so I asked Mrs. Trapini if she could turn down the air conditioning.

"Hey, Mrs. Trapini! Could you do a minor favor and turn down the air conditioning?" I asked.

"Sorry! It doesn't go down."

I groaned loudly. I angrily left her and started to look for Violet. How is the air conditioning unable to go down? It obviously can; she is lying. I saw her turn on her computer with the charger in the corner. She always forgets to charge her laptop, with it barely surviving every day. Has it ever died? I don't know, but it would be unlucky for her if it did. I rapidly approached Violet until I came behind her to tap her shoulder. It would be a lie if I told you she didn't jump.

"Oh my god! You scared me," she exclaimed, shaking her head. "That was the tenth time today!"

"Oh, sorry. I had to show you this." I showed

Violet my paper with ideas for revenge.

"Hmm, the best revenge would be five and seven. They are both similar. Did you forget four is illegal?" She chuckled.

I reread five and seven, and I nodded in approval.

"I honestly believe five would be the best. Becoming friends and stabbing her in the back is the best revenge."

"You're right. I have a plan in mind. You could become friends with her and tell me everything you hear for now. If she ever has something like a party, you could expose her! If she says something rude about her boyfriend, you could record her. I would prefer to stay on the sidelines," Violet felt confident.

"Uhh, there's no way that I'm doing this."

"Come on!"

"Why?"

"You'll become popular!"

Those words sold it for me.

I sighed and gave in.

At the time, I wasn't ready for how much drama this would cause.

"How will I become friends with her?" I solemnly asked.

"Buy her something expensive, transform your look.

There are a lot of things you can do. Besides, you look so ugly. You will never even get through the first step with those clothes. Why are your eyelashes so low!? Fix yourself, and you'll easily become friends."

"Got it! Thanks, Violet! Anyway, I have some work to do. See you soon!"

"Bye," she responded. This is a superb plan. It would be a commendatory idea to start tomorrow. Today would be too recent since she had an affair with us. She has so many incidents every day. She will forget about ours quickly.

Revenge is something that takes over your mind. Something we all have to avoid. What our parents wished we would never think about. There's one thing about it that we wanted would never happen.

We never wanted to be the victim.

But we all need to remember that everything comes back to you. It's karma, and it's either our best friend or our worst nightmare. I will be the karma for Vanessa. She will get every single bit of karma she deserves. I will personally hand her a platter full of her actions. I will give her everything she has done to everyone else. And I mean *everything*.

Life is short. We have to treasure the time we have, and with that time, we have to take risks. This plan is the most significant risk I've ever tried to take. I have to stay low and be secretive. This could make or break me.

You better buckle up.

This story is about to get dangerous.

When I arrived home, I knew I had to become friends with her first. As usual, I walked inside and waved to Mom, who looked cheerful. I didn't want to improvise at the scene, so I made a plan.

I knew I must become friends with her first, so I brainstormed ways to become friends with her. Soon, I had a horrible blister on my middle finger. When I was little, I didn't know how to grip a pencil correctly. I used my middle finger as an extra support for my pencil. If I want to write neatly, I have to write hard. And I mean hard. So, every time I write, my finger has this blister, and it hurts. I have to squish the sides of my finger for it to be better. I've tried to fix it, but I can't, or my handwriting will look like a first grader's. It's too late to fix it. I made my sacrifice. I blew on it a few times, and it started to get slightly better.

I know there is one thing I have to do, and that is to change my looks. Yeah, I used to be confident.

But this is war, and you can't expect your side to win without training.

That evening, I searched for the latest beauty

trends, clothes, and styles. It took me a few hours, but I succeeded. When I go to school, I have the craziest haircut, with all my ends going wrong. I straightened it, curving all the ends toward my chin. Yes, I am supposed to have a bob cut. I looked in the mirror, realizing how pretty I looked. I looked like a strange, new Monica. I could see myself changing, but I hope it's for the better.

I looked at my plain wardrobe, trying to find the prettiest clothes. I searched for an hour, digging inside my tiny boxes full of clothes and my bar full of hangers. The explosion of color started to make me dizzy.

My hands began to tire, so I became lazy and dumped all my clothes. I searched the giant pile, eventually settling on a short, plaid black skirt with white shorts underneath. This might become my favorite skirt, with the soft texture lightly touching my legs. The shorts were comfortable, allowing me to move freely. I found a short top with a checkered design, which reminded me of chess. I laid it on my bed and felt quite tired, so I went to sleep.

The following day, I was prepared. After much self-doubt, I decided to put on a green necklace with tiny stars around it. I put on a few bracelets as well. I didn't want to change my earrings. After putting on my clothes, I walked into the bathroom to put on some cream. My mom begged me to wear it for weeks, but I always forgot. She would be surprised to see me wear it. I walked out and went to my side table. I grabbed some lip gloss, delicately smothering it on my lips. I went into the bathroom and looked into the mirror, shocked by my transformation. I fluffed up my hair and went outside my room to walk downstairs.

✧ ✧ ✧

I was a hot topic at school. All the boys were staring at me, wondering about my transformation. I strutted down the hall, looking for Violet. Did I change that much from one night? Why does everyone love me now? Was I that weird back then? What will happen now?

I still feel like a nerd. Has my rank changed?

I couldn't find Violet, and the bell rang, so I had to bounce to class. Language arts was full of boredom, and I had to use the bathroom. I kindly asked Mrs. Hamlet to go, and she gave me a thumbs up. I exited the classroom, accidentally slamming the door. I calmed down from the jumpscare and started walking to the bathroom.

When I entered, I saw Violet doing her hair. She literally dropped her hairbrush when she saw me.

Why did she bring a hairbrush to school?

She did a double take, thinking she was hallucinating at my appearance.

"Monica? Is that y-you?"

"Who else would it be?" I winked.

"Wow. Anybody would die to be friends with you for that look! I wouldn't be surprised if every boy wants to date you for clout."

"Thanks, I guess? Wouldn't that mean people only like me for my looks?"

"That's why people love celebrities and popular students. For their looks."

Uhh, what? I slowly walked away from her, with my hands in a pushing motion. Is that true? I mean, what about singers? They have talent. People like their singing. That's why they're famous.

Oh god, I'm weird.

After I did my business—with Violet still in the bathroom—I returned to the classroom, with everyone working silently.

When the class finished, I had to go to history class. We all know how Violet is in my class, but there is another person, Vanessa. As she entered class, I could smell her strong perfume. I swished my hand to push away the smoke. How many sprays did she use? Ten-thousand? She looked at me, so I smiled and winked at her. I did a shy wave, wiggling my fingers. I kept walking, trying to look like a confident model simultaneously.

It's so hard to constantly strut. And Vanessa does it in heels!?

I sat next to Violet since we didn't have any assigned seats. I recognized her short, black hair and her tiny height. Surprisingly, the lecture wasn't too boring because we're starting a new unit about the Great Depression. My interest in learning about people who suffered is concerning. Mrs. Trapini gave us an assignment afterward, so I grabbed my favorite mechanical pencil to create it. It has 0.7 lead, my best friend. Any lead thinner than that breaks too easily. The way the company made the pencil is sophisticated, with the inside reasonably visible. I have been thinking about using a mechanical pencil with two-millimeter lead. They look like good-quality pencils, and they don't break easily.

I was happily working on the assignment when Vanessa looked slightly irritated with the work. She was clacking her long black nails on the desk. A few drops of sweat were on her forehead, slightly affecting her makeup.

Oo, a weakness!

Everyone has one.

So I thought, why not try to work my magic? I

patted her on the shoulder, and she questionably turned to me.

"Do you need any help? You look a little confused with the work."

She paused for a moment. Then, she gazed at me in a malicious, manipulative manner.

"Actually, I would love some help! I am severely struggling on the topic, and I would love for you to help me with these problems."

She acted sincere, as if she had never done a single bad thing. It was like she was an undercover devil acting like they were from heaven.

"Which problems do you need help with?" I asked.

"All of them."

Surprised by her immediate response, I was taken aback and shifted myself. After 10 minutes of helping her, I realized she knew nothing about the topic. Honestly, I don't think she paid attention to the lecture. She must've used her phone the entire time. Well, that has its consequences. I must have been so interested in listening to Mrs. Trapini's words that I didn't realize what she was doing. I ignored her actions.

While helping her, I pointed my mechanical pencil at number seven, and she was texting someone on her phone again. She was giggling and chuckling, and it started getting annoying.

"Do you still want my help? Or do you understand everything?" I asked softly. I didn't want to attack her. You can't attack someone like Vanessa Blackmore. That would've been offensive.

"No, no, I think I'm okay now." She immediately returned to her phone. I returned to my seat and sat down with all my work completed.

What?

I didn't complete everything! I barely had three problems done! I was wondering what happened, and Violet winked at me. She must've done the work.

"Thanks, Violet!"

"Anytime," she approved.

I went on my phone, excited to use the beautiful internet. I was fatigued by assignment after assignment. I stumbled upon a video of a comedy skit that was a little funny. I lightly giggled from the video.

When the bell rang, I was about to leave when I saw Mrs. Trapini put both hands on Vanessa's desk. She didn't look too delighted.

"Mrs. Blackmore, you don't have any assignments completed. If you keep this inexcusable behavior, you must repeat the history year."

Her face was in utter shock. I had never seen

Vanessa this way, and it had a whole new effect on me and my perception of her.

"Y-you can't do this!"

"I don't make the rules; I enforce them." She left her in a cast-down way, changing my mood. I rushed outside, hoping she didn't notice me. I urgently sprung to Violet, slightly anxious about what I would tell her. I went right next to her and lightly patted her shoulder. She didn't notice, so I kept doing it until she acknowledged me. Mom hated it when I did that. She says that it is the most irksome trait about me. She looked at me, wondering what I was about to say. I think I jumpscared her. She stared at me, horrified.

"Oh my god, you scared me half to death! What the hell is it?"

"So, I might've, maybe, sorta saw Mrs. Trapini talking to Vanessa. She wasn't pleased. Vanessa has so many missed assignments that she would have to redo the year if she didn't finish them!"

"Oh my god. This is great!"

"It is. Luck must be on our side."

I was jumpy about what happened and how she would get karma. I told you everything you do comes back to you.

We were about to walk to class when Vanessa

tapped me on the shoulder.

"Hey, Monica! Could you help me with history?"

✧ Chapter Eight ✧

So that's her secret. She blackmails people to help her with her studies while focusing on being popular and preppy. I still can't believe this plot has been working since seventh grade! Well, let me rephrase that.

Was working.

"Oh, I would love to help you! Could I give you my number?" I might have been soft on the outside, but a whole new form of rage was boiling inside me.

"Right! Here it is," her tone suddenly changed from kind and innocent to devious and dark. She thought she was one step ahead of me. But it's the opposite.

I'm one step ahead of her.

"Great!" We both had each other's numbers and contact. We both stood there amused. We had to go to our next class, and I can't believe I'm saying this, but it was irritating how we weren't together. I never thought a nerd like me would be delirious from being away from a popular girl. The rest of my classes are with her, so it isn't too much of a problem. Sadly, we're about to go to my worst subject, art. Mom had always told me to worry about studies, not art. She says it is a lousy subject since it "doesn't make too much money." Art seems like a fun career. Doesn't happiness matter more than pay? I am not going to lie. I would like to go down in history as a famous artist. You know, maybe get my art crowned in a museum.

The point is I am as artistic as a raccoon. I don't know how to paint, and I don't know how to draw.

When I was 10, I tried digital art and failed miserably. I thought art was a neat skill to have. I wanted to impress so many people with it. Boy, was I wrong. My pieces were utter trash. I shaded the hair horribly and watched hundreds of tutorials to improve it. In the end, I still couldn't do it. I quit, angry at how bad I was, never to be confident in art again.

Then again, someone like me would never be skilled at it. I guess it's in my genes. All I'm meant for is studying.

Life isn't fair. Everything we want doesn't come to us. I wish it did.

When I was little, I dreamed of a genie almost every night. I thought the genie came to me while in bed, and it would give me three wishes. I would always wonder what my wishes should be. I knew one of them would be for me to have a secret credit card. It would allow me to buy anything I wanted without anyone knowing. My second wish would be that I was the most astute person alive, able to answer any question.

I don't know what my third wish would be.

I was quickly defeated, remembering five seconds later that genies aren't real. I would want to punch something with my anger, wishing life was that easy. It took a few years to realize it wasn't.

The art teacher's name is Mrs. Cotherman. Is it just me, or do art teachers make everything look so easy, but you fail miserably when you try it? Her classroom has paint splattered everywhere, even on the floor. It smells strongly like paint and has art from students all over the walls. The drawings were so skilled. They were from people who donated their artwork to her. People loved the art teacher like their parents. I don't see anything unique about her. She is the average art teacher. Out of all the past teachers I've had, this one is no different. There were countless plastic cabinets on the walls, each holding art supplies. A few cabinets were dedicated to markers, a few were for oil pastels, and some were for clay. There might be a few supplies that I'm forgetting. There are square tables, each holding four people. The seats were uncomfortable stools. Our class was small, so most tables held three people for space. The tables were full of colorful rainbow stains. There was a giant whiteboard and a projector on top of the board. She wrote on the board with whiteboard markers but mainly used the projector. There were a few quotes around the classroom.

I sat down at my seat, dreading to start. I was tired, so I rested my head on the table. When everyone came in, she started the lesson. She told us we were starting a new lesson. I silently groaned and hit my fist on the table.

"Today, we're going to start clay sculptures!"

We do the same units every year. Ever since I was in kindergarten, we have been doing clay sculptures. I turned to Colette, with whom I hadn't talked too much.

We didn't speak a lot about art either. She was

reticent. This was awkward for being friends.

When Mrs. Cotherman finished her lecture, I went to get some clay. It was a neat block she cut with dental floss. Yes, dental floss. You might think it's a weird tool, but she says it's normal! People can use string or embroidery floss to cut it, but I believe the school uses dental floss because it's cheap.

We were making clay animals, and I wanted to make my favorite animal, a Malayan Flying Fox. These enormous bats are colored to look like foxes, hence the name. They look like beasts when they fly at night. Sometimes, I imagine someone sleeping with an open window, and the fox flies inside their bedroom. It's funny, especially if it happened to someone like Vanessa.

I grabbed my computer and looked up references for my animal. The art teacher demands we bring our computers to every class so we can look for inspiration. I turned to Colette, who acted nerdy as usual. She is more of a nerd than me! Just as I glanced at her, she put her glasses up with her index finger.

"What animal are you doing?"

"I'm doing a spider! You know, they're critical animals for the ecosystem despite being hated by many of us. They-"

She kept going on about spiders. Am I always like

this? Even I wouldn't talk this long! "What animal are you doing?"

"I'm going to make a Malayan Flying Fox, which is basically an oversized bat. With their orange fur, they look like foxes." See? I'm not going on for a while.

We started our models and were supposed to mold the body first. That took me half of the class time, 30 minutes. Either I'm unreasonably sluggish at this, or the body is one of the most intricate pieces of the animal. I wouldn't be surprised if the face is five times harder to mold. When I had a decent body, I went on to the face, which I dread.

It had a lot of intricate details, like the tiny pupil for the eyes. I used a toothpick for that and had to draw thin lines to act as fur. The mouth was one of the most complex parts. It connected to the nose with two lines, similar to a lion or cat.

It took a while, but I did finish the whole piece. Mrs. Cotherman assured me that we would paint it in the next class. What!? We literally started the project today!

It was mainly rushing that barely allowed me to finish it. The stress of getting your work done late is a massive fear of mine. It shows teachers that you are irresponsible. I don't want that.

At home, I felt useless. I felt like my life had no point. It was missing something. I felt sick, depressed, a bowl of nothing.

Until I remembered.

Squash. Not the vegetable, but the sport. It's the best! And today we have our lesson! I was so moody before, so bored. Today would be fun for me.

I ran upstairs to change, and Mom noticed me.

"Why are you so happy?" She observed my mood.

"Today we have squash, remember?"

She checked the time and looked worried.

"Oh no! We have to leave soon. Get ready, scat, whatever!"

I didn't hear her last words. I was already upstairs in my room. I put on a shirt, shorts, and my most comfortable socks. They are like 600-thread-count bed sheets for your feet! I sprinted outside my room, holding on to the rail. My hand was being dragged as I was running. I stomped downstairs by accident, each step being louder than the next. I jumped at the last step, eager to leave the boring home.

I couldn't find her, so I looked out the window and saw her in the car. I took a few steps back and looked at the analog clock. I stood in surprise to find it was time to leave. I dashed outside to see Mom waiting for me in the car. She didn't look pleased.

She focused on my expression and gazed at me bitterly. We were silent on the ride to the gym. I was thankful Mom didn't say anything about my tardiness. She must have been too disappointed in my behavior to debate it. When we arrived, there was a demented amount of cars scurrying to find a parking space. There was a corner that was very far away from the gym. And if the whole corner was full of vehicles, then it's crowded. Today was one of those days where we were lucky enough to find an acceptable parking spot. It was a little far away from the entrance to the gym, but hey, isn't that more exercise?

When she saw the spot, she had to straighten the car, although it was already straight. Moms take way too long to park. It's a straightforward action with your car.

She told me to remove her purse, even though she didn't need it. It is not like she will dance with her purse.

My Mom takes the dance class, and I play squash simultaneously. It isn't as disturbing as it sounds. The dance class is right across the three courts. The hallway has the courts and the dance class next to each other, so you can easily watch people. Listening to deafening music while playing a game can be vexatious and delightful at the same time. Usually, we can't hear it, but sometimes the worst thing can happen when one disrespectful dance class person leaves the door open. It might not look like a big deal, but then the lyrics are blasting in our ears. It makes it vigorous to play and makes us lose focus. Thankfully, it doesn't happen frequently.

When we entered, we had to go up these spiral stairs. It had a gray railing that this employee named Paul had redesigned. Paul is a cool guy. He works at the front desk and acts kind to all the customers. He always waves when we enter and leave, saying good night and good morning. It flatters me. A spiral staircase led to the front desk when we entered the gym. They made me feel fancy. When we went to the top of those stairs, we walked through a hallway. There was a left and right side. The left side had four desks that let you sign up for the membership for the gym. The right side had a small seating lounge. If you kept walking, you would get to the front desk, which had a pleasant design. There were stones around the desk, with a blue light around them. They had a calming glow. It made me feel at ease, and Mom walked to this woman named Maisie. We've never seen her at the desk. We knew her name by reading her name tag. She must be a new worker at the gym. It was slightly disheartening to see that Paul wasn't there, but hey, life isn't fair.

She scanned her membership, and the scanner flashed a vibrant green light. It was approved. Mom asked for a few meager towels. He handed them to her, and she aggressively took them.

The stairs led to two areas. The left led to the squash courts, while the right led to the café. The café gave me nostalgia. When I was little, Mom bought me a popsicle if I played well. It wasn't if I only missed a few shots. It was only if I played outstandingly, like one of the professionals. The professionals played like legends. My coach is one of them, and his name is Coach Ikram Khan.

One day, Coach Ikram told me to watch him play. He is a legendary player. He was playing with one of the professionals named Rob. Rob hit the ball in my direction, which was rough and flat. It was breathtaking. Despite the glass barrier, I genuinely thought the ball was coming in my direction. It was flying at the speed of light. I ducked and ran in the other direction. The ball bounced off the glass, which headed to the front wall.

Everyone laughed at me, and I started laughing as well to fit in with them.

Awkward.

The sport has one ball and has as many players as you want. As I described, there is a tiny ball, and you must hit it with your racket. It resembles a tennis racket, but the head is shaped like an egg. The sport seems easy, but don't judge a book by its cover! There are many rules with it. You have serving, forehand, backhand, boasts, drop shots, drives, and more! The objective is to hit the ball so the opponent can't hit it back. There is tape on the floor, which indicates the boundaries. There are two sides, which depend on whether you're left or right-handed. There are rules for serving the ball. To serve, one of your feet must be in the box, represented by the tape.

It's a lousy explanation, sorry. But it is not close to emphasizing running and hitting the ball with extreme strength. Don't underestimate it. Try the sport yourself. Then you'll see how difficult it is.

I breezed through the entrance, waving my arms through the hallway. I discovered one free court, so I placed my squash bag on the couch and waved to Mom as she descended to the class. I started my warmup. It's probably the most essential part before playing any sport. Warmup reduces the risk of injury and allows more oxygen inside your arms and legs. It also loosens your joints, enabling you to move freely. I've heard the stories of injuries caused by forgetting to warm up.

When I finished warmup, I went inside the court to start solo. It's where you hit the ball to yourself. It's one of the best things you can do to improve your game.

I served the ball. It proudly went high on the wall. I didn't hit it too hard, giving me enough reaction time to hit it hard. It bounced off, returning to me as planned. The ball gracefully flew to me like a dove flying down a branch. I prepared my racket to hit it. I raised my arm high, ready to strike. The ball came to me like a frisbee. It was about to bounce on the floor, and I took a deep breath to prepare. It bounced, and I put my left foot forward. It was in flawless condition to hit it, so I mentally prepared myself and swung my racket as hard as possible! It was a hard shot, soaring back to the wall and landing exactly where I wanted it to.

Watching my successful shots made me feel thrilled with my effort.

Solo continued until Coach Ikram called me for our lesson. It was an hour of fun. I got out of the court, struggling to open the door. The lock is rusty, and it takes a lot of work to open. There are times when I can't even open it. Sometimes, I have to lean and put my weight on the lock. Even that might not budge it open!

It isn't a huge deal. It takes a slight but robust tuck.

I got out and went over to his court. I slammed the door shut. It doesn't close quickly. I practiced my racket swing a few times, waiting for him to get the balls. I knew to use the tips he told me, and they made a swoosh with the air. You know your shots are hard when you hear a swoosh from your swing. The louder the swoosh, the more rigid the swing. They were pretty loud, so I credited myself.

When he came in, I prepared my body for his swing. He can hit a shot at any moment and expect me to hit it. Then, he would give me a look of disappointment since I missed it. He would tell me what we would do and give me another ball in a split second. Luckily, I'm used to it and quickly hit it.

I would recommend you to get used to my lying.

I'll never prepare myself for Coach Ikram's shots.

Ever.

After I missed the shot, he smirked and announced that we would play a game. I became excited. We rarely play games together. Coach Ikram always says I need more practice. Today must allow me to show my skills. I held my racket up in glee. He warmed up the ball with solo, so I practiced my swing a few times. He handed the ball to me when he finished. I'll serve.

I served the ball nice and high. He received it back with a quick shot. It was low, but not low enough! I swung, hitting a shot too low for him to hit, which is a drop shot. As soon as it hit the wall, he stared at me, disappointed as I got the ball.

I snickered as I served the ball again. The score is one-zero. The person who serves has the first set of points. For example, since I won the point, I have one.

The serve was high again, and it hit the back wall. Coach panicked, and he did one of the most revolutionary squash shots. He hit the ball to the back wall with so much force. It flew to the front wall, barely hitting it. I ran toward it and slightly hit the shot so he would have to run to hit it. But I blundered. The shot was too low. It hit the tin, which is a place you can't hit, and I lost the point.

The score is now one-one. Coach Ikram served from the forehand side, so I was on the backhand. He gave me a serve that bounced from the side wall. I hit it straight, so he had to run from the middle to hit it. I gladly took the middle. The middle of the court is the most powerful spot. You control the whole court. He hit the shot to me, so I switched it to the corner again. He didn't have to run. He just lunged to the ball, hitting it faintly. I sprinted to the ball and hit it as hard as possible!

It went to the other side and bounced to the ground. He couldn't hit it and looked at me again in spite.

The game continued until he won. Sure, I had an efficient start, but he is practically unbeatable. I was disappointed I lost, but I know I'll beat him someday.

After the game, he looked at me surprised.

"You did a lot better than I expected," he commented. "I thought you would miss a few serves, but all of them were okay."

"Oh, nice," I responded. I went to get some water since I was quenching my thirst. After I got water, Mom's dance class finished. She walked up to me and said it was time to leave. The lesson had ended at that last game, so I put my racket in my bag and slipped on my jacket. I waited for Mom to get ready, and when she was, we left to go home.

We walked upstairs to the entryway when Mom asked me.

"How did you do?"

"I did well. Today we played a game! I lost 8 to 11. I feel a little sentimental that I lost. Today could've been the day I beat Coach Ikram."

"You have to do better," she murmured.

"How was dance class?" I was eager to ask. Mom

looked tired. She must have worked hard today.

"Today was the best! Darcie moved my row up to second! This means I have improved in dance!"

"That's great!"

We walked out of the gym. When we got out, I jumped in the car, and we drove home.

✧ Chapter Nine ✧

I was resting in bed, looking at my phone. I put it back on my gloomy bedside table, maximizing the volume of my alarm. I started to drowse off when I got a text. I sighed, checking my phone. Due to my rigid sleep, it was 11:30, and I went to bed at nine. Who would be texting me during this hour? I uneagerly inspected my phone. I scrolled through my notifications until I found who had sent the text. It was Vanessa. Why would she text me at such a late time? The text said, "Wanna come to my house on Saturday at 11? You could help me with history and the math homework. We can chill together as well, maybe watch some TV?"

I didn't want to leave her on read, so I messaged her back, being aware of this late time. I responded by saying *I am available on Saturday but must ensure I can come.* She quickly responded, saying, "Finally! Someone who can respond to my texts quickly! Thank god you don't text me back the next day." She doesn't like waiting, showing she is impatient. Her response was a little sassy, but it was Vanessa. You can't expect anything different. I need to think of something clever to text her back.

After heaps of thinking, I sent this: *I don't like to make people wait.*

I'm no expert at texting, but that was a clean answer. I put my phone back just so it could ding again. I whined with sorrow. I know I'm being impatient, but can you let me sleep!? It's 11:30 p.m. I'm tired. I had an exhausting day. I examined the text, and she replied with a thumbs-up emoji. I sincerely wanted to sleep, so I texted *night*. Thankfully, she texted night as well, so I exhaled in relief. I raised my phone volume, placed it on my bedside table, and dozed off.

✧ ✧ ✧

I walked into school, aware that today was the most overrated day of the week, Friday. I like Friday, but by definition, it is overrated. It's overrated since too many people like it and too few dislike it.

Ugh, you're being nerdy again, Monica! You have to stop this, remember?

I kept my stylish look, getting everyone's kind-of frightening attention. I knew I had to hide my true feelings, so I waved and smiled at everyone. I stayed silent like a black cat.

Superstitions ruined those cats. Black cats are normal, but nobody likes them because they are "bad luck." According to research, black cats are playful and full of energy. They must be the least adopted cats in shelters.

There was a little time before the bell rang, so I looked through my locker, making sure I had all my materials and books. After checking it six times, I was sure I had everything I needed. I shut my locker to be greeted by Drew standing on the other side of the door. I nearly fell, taking a few deep breaths. Breathe in, breathe out.

"What do you want? You scared me half to death!" He could see my irritation.

"Oh, uhh, hey. What's up?" He was leaning at the side of someone's locker. They were trying to get through.

"What's up? You scared me so bad!"

"Oh, yeah. Goodbye."

He walked off like he didn't do anything. I stood there, confused, wondering what had just happened. Why did he do that? I watched him go away, and he went to Chad, hitting him and being flustered. He was tapping his shoulder like a demented person in an insane asylum. Having no idea what happened, I went to look for Violet. She was at her locker, getting a few books. I snuck up on her and hugged her when I was behind her. She slowly leaned herself into my hug, closing her eyes. I remembered that I needed to tell her about my messages with Vanessa. She paused momentarily, finally asking me why I hugged her.

"Why are you hugging me?" She inquired.

"I have something crucial to tell you."

"What is it?"

"Vanessa messaged me yesterday at 11:30 p.m. We had a rather brief conversation, but she asked me if I wanted to come to her home on Saturday. Should I go?"

"Of course! Is that even a question? Make sure to tell me every detail!"

"I wouldn't be surprised if she has the richest mansion here."

I texted Vanessa, saying that I could come.

That was a late response.

We stood silent for a moment, thinking. I left Violet, and the bell rang a few moments later. I went to language arts, feeling bummed.

✧ ✧ ✧

On Saturday, I checked the time, and it was 10:30, so I asked Mom to take me to Vanessa's home. She gladfully agreed, wondering how much I'd changed these past weeks. Why is she taking care of herself? Is she being bullied? Is she being forced to change due to specific standards? Maybe my current situation is a combination of all three.

When I saw her home, I gasped at its beauty. It was a pure mega mansion the size of a city—the most extensive home I've ever seen! I don't know how she navigates it; I would be lost in there.

I got out of the car and waved to Mom. She opened her window, wanting to say something.

"Be safe! Have fun, and make sure to call me!"

"I got it!" She drove off, and I eagerly walked over to the entrance. It is composed of a few steps that lead to the door. I walked up those steps feeling like a queen. It had a keypad to her home and a speaker button. Weirdly, there was no doorbell, so I clicked the speaker button, hoping she could hear me.

"Oh, uh, hey, Vanessa! You invited me to come to your home yesterday. So, can I, like, come in? Can you even hear me? Sorry, my home isn't as prestigious as yours. It doesn't have all of these graceful features."

The doors opened, and I walked in with a warm breeze. The sudden warmth from the sheer cold outside gave me chills. I gazed at the marble statues. The statues were an exact replica of Vanessa. Her luscious hair and legendary cheekbones were on the statue. The statue had her most infamous outfit on it. Talk about a narcissist.

A grand staircase was in front of me, with two C-shaped stairs and a circular carpet between them. I wondered which direction to walk in, left or right. I stood there and stumbled when Vanessa appeared out of nowhere!

"You like my home?" She asked, her facial expression telling me she knew the answer. I could tell she loved her home. Imagine if she lost all her money and everything there was gone. All her designer bags and jewelry would disappear, as her dad would have to sell them. The makeup and constant haircuts every day would fade away.

"Like it? I love it! Look at the sheer excellency at this entrance and the exterior! Your home is so fancy that it doesn't have a doorbell. It has a freaking recorder-voice-thingy. The sheer beauty of the home is staggering!" I added more expression and adjectives to my speech to show how much I loved it. She smiled warmly and told me to walk with her. Since I will help her with history, I should ask her questions about it.

"What do you need help with in history?"

"Everything," she quickly responded.

"Okay," I muttered.

We kept walking until we arrived at this giant room. The door had a massive picture of Vanessa's face. Her face. There was a ton of pink fuzz rimming the ends of the picture. A light pink garland surrounded the door rim. The doorknob was glazed with a shiny golden metal. It had a black happy face on it with clear visibility. There was a rug that had a weird text. It announced, "Vanessa, the girl everyone wants to be," which was made with high-end fabric. The rug's colors were the same as usual: pink and purple. She smirked at me and opened the door. The room was filled with the smell of alcohol.

Ester was sitting on the bed.

"Yeah, we both need help with history."

I took a deep breath, unaware the person who punched me would be in this room—Vanessa's evil best friend, who wanted me to disappear into a black hole.

That includes the process of spaghettification, but we won't talk about that torture.

Why didn't she tell me that she was coming? Oh, classic Vanessa! I tried not to look at her, knowing she would give me a death threat. Maybe she would move her finger against her neck, threatening to slice my head off. Agony filled me. The fear of being harassed again was painful to me.

Her dark and antagonizing smirk was making me tremble.

Then I realized I didn't have to do this without a *price*. You cannot help someone without getting anything back!

"Vanessa, I won't help you without a price."

She turned her head in a surprised motion.

"A price, hmm? Oh, I got it! Will a few thousand be okay for this lesson?"

She said that, acting as if it was customary for someone to offer that much money. Her sassy tone increased when she said that.

"I like a few thousand, but there is something more important than that. A certain necklace."

She stared at me, shocked at the preposterous words that came out of my mouth.

"Uhh, fine, I guess." She said with an annoyed tone.

Hah, touché! She rolled her eyes and sprinted to her closet. She threw the necklace at me. I posed in victory.

She whispered something to Ester, covering her sly mouth with her hand. They were too far away for me to hear it.

I don't want to see that sly mouth in action.

There were alcohol bottles and a lot of makeup on the side table. All those expensive brands were shining on my face, taunting me. All the luxury makeup was shining on the table. The left side had a wall of purses from the famous brands used to flex. Those brands could make the toughest feel insecure. She wore those purses daily, flaunting and laughing at all the poor kids. She even had one unique purse with the letter V on it. It had a million white gemstones radiating like a disco ball.

She even wore it in math class. Oh, shiver me timbers, Mr. Leslie. Confidence is key, but it is different from being a vulgarian. My eyes waltzed onto the bed, praying there wasn't more pink.

She has a king bed. Mom doesn't even have a king bed. There was a remote next to the pillow. It activated the LED lights on the varnished marble bed rim. The lights were colored, of course, pink, but there were multiple colors on the remote. She did it to match the theme. The mattress was a plaid design, with the background being white. My eyes were blessed to stare at a color different than pink.

The blanket had the most random design.

It literally had a picture of her holding money. What kind of person would take it so far that their mattress is suffering from their face? I wanted to give her a long lecture about sanity, but I knew I couldn't for the good of the school.

There was a table. Not a desk, a full crude table. It was the size of a circular dining table with three chairs. The texture was a lacquered limestone white. It was clean. There were a few textbooks on the table. Okay, maybe they are trying to study. But that was an assumption that would never possibly be true.

The books were opened to the wrong chapter. It wasn't opened at the Great Depression. Oh no, the chapter was opened to the Native Americans.

"Umm, are you trying to learn about the Native Americans?"

"Yeah, isn't that what we're learning?"

I looked at Ester, and she nodded her head.

"We're learning about the Great Depression!" I cried.

"Oh," they admitted with shame.

With heavy-heartedness, I started on the first part

of the Great Depression. It took me an hour to help them understand the first part. The Great Depression was more like The Great Annoyance when I teach them. They drowsed off every few minutes. Did Connor lie? Was I that bad of a teacher?

Life sucks, but teaching people like this is even worse. They stopped paying attention, so I wanted to ask something.

"Do you need a break?" I asked with a dark tone.

"Y-yes," She complained. "All this learning is hurting my head!"

"Hmm. Do you have anything you want to eat?"

She didn't respond, as she was on her phone, giggling while texting someone. I clacked my nails on the table, feeling awkward. Wait a minute. I might be able to figure out some dirt on her...

"Who are you texting?"

"Oh, I'm texting Drew. He told me that he'll buy me a special bag!"

"He is your boyfriend, correct?"

"Yep."

"Do you love him?"

"Hah! No way. He can buy me anything."

"Aren't you rich?" I moved my hands around the room, emphasizing her fortune.

"Yeah, but a few extra bucks never hurt anyone." Her intrusive thoughts took her over. I sucked my teeth, hearing she was using him. I almost felt sympathy for him, but he punched me. I need to stop holding grudges. Get over it. It was the past.

"Say, who do you like?" Vanessa was curious.

"Oh, I don't have a crush," I calmly replied.

"Aren't you always with Connor?" Ester wondered.

Her question was sharp, piercing me in the heart.

"He," I didn't have an adequate answer. What should I say? Anything I respond with will make Vanessa raise an eyebrow. I am trying to help him with work. All of us were silent for a few seconds.

"Awkward," Vanessa mumbled.

Did we ask for your opinion?

No.

I could tell Ester despised me. Her bitter looks and hateful actions were clearly visible to most of us, and my flurry of thoughts started to flow toward them.

"To be fair, he is kinda hot," Vanessa announced.

"She may have a taste for men," Ester murmured.

Why would Vanessa date Drew if she likes Connor?

"Wait a minute. Do you like Connor?"

"He isn't that ugly, but I can't date him."

"Why?"

"Isn't it obvious? My popularity will disappear like a deflated balloon. Similar to what happened to dumb Colette," Vanessa declared.

"Wait a minute, are you saying that Colette used to be popular!?"

"Correction: she was almost popular. She would've become the best of the best, but she didn't pass the final test. Oh, and those glasses?! No way. She could never pull it off," Vanessa corrected.

There's a test!? Paper or digital?

"Wow..."

"That's all she gets to know," Vanessa whispered to Ester, and they fist-bumped. The secrets these two keep are like one colossal puzzle. I have to crack the code. The thing is, I have to find out how to tell everyone—not just the people she has affected.

Oh no, I mean the whole school.

I have to find a way to expose her in a way the entire school will hear. I'm not saying that we have to spread gossip the usual way. We need a tool to tell everyone. How about a loudspeaker?

I will need to think when I have more information. This is my first time seeing them, but it won't be the last.

Their ego is unnaturally high and sharp like a knife. They block out everyone in their path, the traits you don't want. They assume their life is flawless, with everyone loving them like a celebrity. However, celebrities have haters. They don't know their lives aren't remarkable, giving everyone's standards to be like them. I cannot imagine their fear of losing all they have: their popularity. I don't want to remind them of their desperate need for help in history. Should I remind them that we need to resume studying? Will they call me a nerd? Something as simple as this could remove my hope to be friends with them.

Life has no room for breaks. Work, work, work, and you will get a reward. We have to go through 12 years of a system known as "school." A land full of hatred, fear, and pressure. Most people recieve a degree worth their life, and we need it for a job. We work until retirement, where we finally get our well-deserved break. That's how Mom planned my dull life, where I receive a master's degree in Computer Science. She says I need to be rich.

That's how my life was supposed to turn out. But it has a plot twist. One that could have a trail of fear. If I mess up, the rest of my life will be destroyed. It would remove all of my hope for a decent future. It's a game of chess against Vanessa. She's *Stockfish*, and I'm a beginner.

I finally decided to ask them.

"Would you like to resume studying?"

"Meh, I feel like a drink."

Vanessa walked up to her table, eager to drink. Suddenly, she grabbed the bottle and popped the cork open. The label said it was vodka. Reading each letter made me more sick of her drinking. Does she realize that this is illegal? People in the United States can drink at the age of 21. She's 17! This one action could take her life away!

She drank a sip, feeling so relieved.

"Y-you do realize this is illegal, right?"

"Who's going to realize? Unless you snitch."

"E-Ester, do you drink?!"

"Yeah, all the time."

"Would you like to try some?" Vanessa inquired.

"No, I'm f-fine, thank you." I quickly denied the request.

"Meh, she'll be drinking in a few weeks," Vanessa mumbled to Ester.

They both chuckled, aware of my fate.

✧ Chapter Ten ✧

On Monday at school, I felt as if I hadn't uncovered enough information when I met with Vanessa. Time is of the essence, and I can't waste it. I need to see her again as fast as possible. I went to Violet, and she seemed to be looking for me. Her anguished face showed it all. She looked the same at first, but I found what had changed. Her hair was dyed purple, and she received a lot of compliments. The ends of her hair had purple tips. I thought it looked diverting on her. She has never dyed her hair, so I wonder what has caused her to change. I was walking to her, but Connor approached me.

"How is it going?"

"Amazing!" I left my walk to Violet to talk with him amongst ourselves. "So, do you need help with anything?"

"I don't need too much help with any subject."

"You say *too much help*. That means you still need it. One quick session could make you fluent in every subject. I could do a check-up as well."

"How could I say no to you?" He made me blush. "We meet tomorrow?"

"That's okay for my schedule."

His sweet voice and calm personality gave me chills. He is cool.. I pity him, losing his popularity. With a tiny scene, all he had worked for was gone. But he is different. He's trying to fix himself. I've seen so many students lose their popularity. Out of all those kids, he is the only one improving himself. The rest lost everything else, one by one. Their friends and family left them like their hope for love.

The bell rang, so I went to language arts. Nothing new happened there, so I will skip to history.

Vanessa looked sly and excited. She stopped using her phone and tucked it into her pocket. It's like she wants to pay attention to the class. She curled her hands and placed them on the desk like a gentleman, or woman in this case. I've never seen Vanessa maintain her composure this well. If she participates in the class, which is very unlikely, will I be the one to thank? Will she credit me while answering a question? I hope not. What if she gets the question wrong? My relationship with her should be kept secret. She would be the one to know that. I must be paranoid. The best thing to do is to hide myself, to stay in the shadows. I nudged myself under the desk. I have to remain unnoticed. There aren't any assigned seats in this class, so I will sit in the back. Do any of Vanessa's friends know about her past? It must have been messy to be so corrupted. Her life will be ruined after high school, but she is unaware of it. Willow Creek was her peak, and it will all go down. Will she even go to college? As the lesson went on, I realized she was listening! Unbelievable! She learned something while I was teaching her! This experiment was a success! I cheered in my mind, surprised that someone had listened to me. But this wasn't someone. This was the most popular student in the school! I was honestly shocked she cared. I thought she invited me to flex her home and family name. Her last name, Blackmore, is famous. Her father owns a jewelry brand called "Blackmore's Best!" She has told everyone a million times. I have been to the store once, and let me tell you, it is so expensive. Fifty dollars for a pair of earrings! Hundreds of dollars for a necklace!

Oh, I need a break. I am overreacting. But I can't take a break. As I told you before, life doesn't allow for breaks. What should I do? I can't believe I have been on the plan for a few days and am already exhausted. I must be going crazy. The pressure of all these things going wrong in my mind makes me go insane. I need to take a break. Life has been getting so hard. With all this sudden pressure from Mom, acing all my high school classes, participating in extracurriculars, and helping the school, I feel like my life will never have fun. My only natural talent has been wasted and thrown in the trash.

This is unacceptable. I don't even think reading will help!

The one thing that blessed my life won't help me.

When will this wretched curse called life end?

✧ ✧ ✧

My sanity was barely intact as I panicked about what to do. I'm sorry for confusing you. I was puzzled as well. I didn't understand what was happening, even though there was a clear and straightforward solution.

I know what to do. I have a plan, and it is flawless in my eyes. This will solve all of the problems. I will maintain everything I have, and everyone will worship me. All I wished for will come true.

All I have to do is *act like Vanessa*. By acting like her, I mean acting stylishly and classily. I have to stop being the old Monica. I have to be a new, improved version. I haven't been taking that too seriously. I need to be mysterious in a clever way. I have to stop being a nerd. I have to become a true popular girl.

I should give it a try. You never know if something is good if you don't try it! If it doesn't work, then I'll stop.

❖ ❖ ❖

It was Tuesday, the day I met with Connor to help him study. I didn't feel like going to school, and my mental happiness was going down. There were butterflies in my stomach, and they turned to dragons. I wanted to leave the world and imagined my joy if I lost my gravity. I would fly into space, never having to deal with drama again. The brittle feeling of going to hell every day isn't too relaxing. There was a student I knew, Sapphire, who was the worst. Every day, she would complain to all her friends about her horrible life. She always talked about her name being a jewel when nobody cared. Her friends eventually left her, delirious of her need for pity.

Do you want to know about her life? She had a hefty home that was bigger than most. Her wealthy parents bought her anything she wanted. She could buy the *Mona Lisa* with the snap of her fingers. When I came to high school, she was a junior, but even the freshmen heard her bickering. Her friends dumped her during lunch, and everything went downhill.

Now that I had to act like Vanessa, I also had to be like her at home. On Tuesday, my mood was low, so I lied to Mom. I told her that I was sick. Before, I wouldn't do that, but I've changed. And let me tell you, it was amazing!

I can't believe I didn't skip school before! Honestly, who cares if I miss one day of school? I was so nerdy and bulky back then.

A break is a break. I mainly rested for the whole day on my favorite armchair. Mom delivered me soup and lentils. The aroma of the fresh soup gave me chills. It was like she was my butler for the whole day. I acted like a damsel in distress, complaining about every minimal thing. I worked on one minor assignment so I could fully unwind. To relax is a new feeling, where I don't have to worry.

I rested for hours, thankful I didn't have to go to that cursed land. At five, I had to go to Connor's home. When it was an hour before I had to leave, I started to get ready. The cracks I heard after I got up from the chair were uncanny.

I went to Mom and told her that I would see a school friend. She approved and asked me what time we had to leave. When I finished telling her about the information, I went to get ready, just when she realized my mistake. It was at the last second that she developed the suspicion.

"I thought you were sick?"

"I feel better now."

"Are you sure?" She appeared skeptical.

"Yes, I'm okay!" I was a little demanding and tense.

"Hmm, fine, I guess." Mom left, making me a little anxious. Will this work? Her awful look evoked a variety of emotions, but joy wasn't one of them.

I decided to wear my favorite clothes there. After all, you have to look professional. I chose to wear a soft, bright pink top with flowers. The flowers were daisies, giving me a peaceful vibe. I decided to wear a dark pink skirt to contrast with the bright pink. I know it's better to wear a dark shade of a color than black. White goes well with pink, so I wore white tights.

One problem: I hate tights. They are so itchy and take so long to put on. I know I have to look fancy, so I have to suck it up. I brushed my hair (thank god I did; it had so many knots) and ate a mint. The crisp taste of the mint freshened my breath. I got some of Mom's cream and aggressively smothered it on my face. I was thinking about makeup, but it was a heavy risk. I've never used makeup and don't want to look like a clown. Looks can jeopardize friendships. You could be friends with someone for years, and they could leave you because you looked freaky that day. The fear of someone leaving you for someone better is frightening. You need to eliminate all the threats. That's what Vanessa did, and look at her now—loved by all, elegant, whimsical, *ludicrous*. I don't want to lose him as well.

When we left, I saw Mom's thinking face. She furrowed her eyebrows and bit her lower lip. It was a little silly. When I was six, I would laugh hysterically every time she made that face. I gazed at it, thinking of old memories. I was silent until I decided to use my phone. I scrolled and scrolled until I encountered a droll video. I guffawed, and Mom noticed.

"What are you watching?" Mom snapped.

"Nothing," the word slipped out of my mouth.

"Tell me. Are you texting someone?"

"I'm not texting anyone! Mind your own business."

She gasped at my comment and looked at me. I knew she would give me the "don't speak to your Mom like that" attitude, but she was reticent instead. Back then, I wasn't expected to laugh like that while on my phone. She said that as a family, we have to tell each other everything. We trust each other! I was confused but secretly thankful she didn't say anything.

When we arrived, I waved goodbye, and Mom didn't wave back. She drove off, stomping on the gas pedal. I turned around to look at the home, and my jaw dropped.

His home wasn't a home. It was a recreational vehicle. It was puny, being smaller than a public restroom. There were two clerestory windows. How does his whole family live there? I forced myself to become as serene as possible. I slowly walked to the door, hoping he wouldn't mention anything about his home. I kept repeating to myself to act as normal as possible. How was he so popular when he had a home like this!? (Not to offend anyone). Did he never invite anyone to his home? Did he make up any excuse he could think of? Did they use him for his knowledge? Wait, of course not. He was stupid before I started helping him. Did they like him since he was so athletic? Is that why they abandoned him so quickly?

There was no doorbell, so I knocked on the door with force. Nobody opened the door a few moments later, so I hit harder. The air quality around the home wasn't so pleasant. I kept coughing and coughing. The smell was irritating me. Imagine a rotten sandwich combined with sewage. The "home" walls were a butter yellow with horizontal planks as the walls. The roof was shaped like a trapezoid. There were some daisies around the vehicle, which made me grin. I kept patiently waiting, and someone came to the door. Oh, but it wasn't Connor.

A weird man with a wacky haircut was standing there. His hair was sticking up, and he had a unibrow. He had these geeky glasses that had square lenses. He had a mustache that was shaped precisely like a rectangle. He was wearing a white tank top and bulky black shorts. His ears were sticking out. I got a few goosebumps!

"Oh, uhh, hey, are you Connor's friend?"

"Uhh, yeah."

"He is, uhh, coming in a minute. How are you doing today?"

"Good, I guess."

"You want to come over so-"

"Hi, Monica! Sorry, this is my dad. Do you want to come inside?" Connor interrupted him. Thank god he did. I don't think I wanted his father to finish that sentence.

"I would love to come in!"

Another reason they dumped him might be because of his father.

I walked in, and the home was spotless. There was one petite bed and one large bed. The petite bed was cluttered, with an unwrinkled blanket. The blanket had a crochet design, almost like someone in the household had made it. It had a chevron design, which was oddly soothing. There was a laptop on top of the blanket, which had a few stickers on the cover. One sticker had a picture of a basketball. The pillows were plain white with no cases. There was a wooden side rim with a lot of scratches. The bed had no back or front board. The large bed was gleaming. It looked like a hotel room bed with white sheets. The bed blanket was tucked in firmly. It reminded me of the struggle of staying in a hotel room and struggling to pull out the bottom sheet. This blanket didn't look homemade. They probably bought it from a store. The kitchen was compact, having every necessity. It had a few counters and a low-quality stove that was greasy. It was dusty, having a few specks of dust on it. There were a few shelves containing some books and plants, and one was dedicated to spices. The plants didn't look very healthy, with each slowly losing their leaves, signaling the cycle of life and death. The living room had two red armchairs and one giant red couch. All of the furniture was the same color. The carpet had an antique design with sunflowers. The television barely fit in the space. A million shelves surrounded the television, full of copies of movies. A collection of the most famous films was dedicated to one shelf, and the rest had extras. It had a label on it saying "Famous Movies," which was unusual. There was a door at the left end. I think that's for the bathroom. The scent wasn't unbearable, so that told me something. There was one table, which was probably for the dining table. It was so bijou and compact. I still can't believe he lives here! I've never met anyone who lives in a drivable home.

Connor kept looking at me, worried. He was sweating, and his actions confirmed it. He scratched his shoe on the floor, and his lip quivered. He took my hand and dragged me to the table. He was tumultuous about seeing me. There were two chairs, one for me and one for him. I steadily sat down, keeping my maturity. He practically jumped on the chair, which was leaning over. It went back to its spot. The chair had a broken piece.

"Can I see your notes?" I need to know if he has been writing everything correctly.

"Of course! They are right here."

He handed them to me. I carefully skimmed each

page, being glad of his neat handwriting. I felt the beautiful feeling of indented words on a page. The written paper relieved me of all my troubles. It reminded me of my lost dream. I looked through them for a few minutes, as there was a big stack. I didn't know he took this much effort for notes. To be fair, our teachers do tell us a lot of information. It is easy to forget everything you learned.

"Your notes have all of the correct information and are spectacular. You make an effort to write everything down. There were a few facts that I couldn't recall!"

"You didn't remember them because you missed school today. There's no way you would forget anything."

"That's very nice of you to say!"

"What can I say? I'm telling the truth!"

"You flatter me."

We kept checking everything, and I assure you everything he had was correct! I learned from him as well. After all, you learn something new every day.

Connor's cool. I want to stay friends with him.

In conclusion, my meeting with him was full of laughter, questions, and suspicious comments from his father.

✧ Chapter Eleven ✧

I walked into school confidently, ensuring *everyone* could see me. I did a hair flip, adoring my long hair. I saw Violet, but instead of approaching her, I went to Vanessa, unwelcome. She saw me coming toward her and started to chuckle.

"Why are you here?" Vanessa demanded to know.

"Isn't it obvious? I want to hang out with you."

"Don't try to fool me, nerd. You could never pull off hanging out with us. You'll end up like Colette."

"Who says I am a nerd? What if I'm a completely new person?"

"How can you prove that?"

"By hanging out with you." She went silent after what I said and whispered something to Ester.

Ester shrugged, having no problem with me. I was a little surprised she did that. Instead of talking, they used their phone the entire time. No, let's not gossip. Let's watch social media and text our boyfriends.

I didn't feel like starting a conversation. I probably wasn't expected to stay with them, so the least I could do was not say anything. Who knows, maybe they were texting someone important. Like their mother, or something. (Who am I kidding, they would never text someone they love.)

When the bell rang, they didn't go to class. They were still texting. I almost reminded them to attend class, but I figured not to. Skipping class once wouldn't be a huge deal. They must do it all the time. That is partially a reason that Vanessa is failing all her classes. They would give me weird looks if I reminded them about class. *I can't believe she is so pretty and cares about learning. What a nerd.*

A few minutes later, they were still there. The teachers would have taken attendance by now. However, they walked away from the spot while I was still standing there, making me rethink if I should do this.

"Well, are you coming? Or are you such a dumbo

that you can only stay with us for five minutes? Are you trying to impress us by barely staying? You can't trick us that easily."

I scurried behind them. They were in the front, and I was in the puny back. They were talking while I was hushed. However, I have to be like Vanessa, so I knew I had to make up something to discuss. Then I got the perfect idea. But first, I had to pull up something to record her speaking. When I pulled it up, I was ready. I kept the recording app on my phone. I was holding it down on the side of my leg.

"Vanessa, do you like Drew?"

"Didn't I tell you that I use him for money? Pay attention more." She scoffed, and I smiled. I turned off my recorder, eager to show Drew. This will be useful later. She thought I was ignorant and never listened to her, but I was just recording her. I wonder what Drew's reaction will be when he sees this. Will he be surprised? Will he care in the first place? Oh, I know what will happen. He will just immediately break up with her!

She kept walking until we were at the school exit.

"Do you want to come with us? Or are you a loser who can't do anything?" Vanessa rolled her eyes, pushed the door open, and left. Vanessa and Ester were laughing while walking. I knew what to do, so I ran behind her.

When I came, she stopped. I didn't see what the problem was. Did she underestimate me? Whatever.

They were whispering to each other about something, and it irks me not to know what it was. Why are they always talking!? It's like someone is speaking about me being annoying in front of my face.

She kept going with Ester. Every step was more and more eerie.

There was a dark alley. It was full of old spiderwebs, and it was super dusty. I started to cough while swaying my hand. Back then, I couldn't fathom going here. Imagine what Mom would think if she saw me. I was quivering. My shaky hand was shining to the stars. The alleyway was grimy. There were dark, murky puddles all over the path. The path was full of sullied cobblestone. It had a few full trash cans. Overall, the area was polluted. I wouldn't be surprised if the trash cans were overflowing for decades. The stench was giving me a headache. It was the worst fume that had ever entered my nose. I groaned, dreading to come with them. I started to feel worried. Are they doing something illegal? Why are they here? Wouldn't their parents be disappointed in their actions? Do they realize these actions will affect their future? *Be like Vanessa* are the three worst words to come to my mind. They were a huge mistake.

When we finished our walk, Vanessa and Ester started to whine. I didn't notice them as I scowled at the grim, languish surroundings. The area could have been so beautiful, but they ruined it. Seeing this area made my blood boil for no absolute reason. Monica, you're being stupid again, aren't you?

Someone finally arrived, and they intimidated me. A five-year-old would run away from someone like this in fear. They'd cry to their mother. *Mommy, help me! I saw the scariest man ever!* He had a black beanie on and a black face mask. His jacket was, you guessed it, black. The only color on him was these blue ripped jeans with a studded belt. Vanessa proceeded toward him.

"About time you came," Vanessa said.

"You got the money?" He inquired.

"Here you go! A thousand, just like you wanted."

His frown slowly turned into a wicked smile. He gave her a bag with bottles of alcohol.

"Thanks. I'll see you *soooon*," Vanessa sang.

"I look forward to doing more business with you," he said, sprinting away. Ester ran toward Vanessa, holding out her smooth hand. Vanessa opened the bag and gave her a bottle.

"You want some? Oh, let me guess, of course not!

You might be slightly brave to come out with us, but there's no way you would take some of this gold. You were trembling when we held some bottles at the party!" At that moment, I had no idea what to do. A variety of emotions circled my head, and my self-esteem quickly lowered. But the words *be like Vanessa* took me over. I had no choice. I had to do it. My social life with them forced me.

"Actually, I would love some ... alcohol." I held out my hand and formed a smirk. She had no idea I would go this far.

"What? Hmm," she murmured. She handed me a bottle of vodka, the strongest alcohol in the world, and I took a few moments to realize what I had done. I have alcohol in my hand. And you want to know the next part? I drank it. It tasted disgusting. It was so strong and bitter. How do people enjoy this? How does this make you feel better from your problems? The energy I had from a few sips was like no amount of coffee. It felt so weird. I can see why it is illegal for people under 21. I can see someone getting addicted to this. Why would someone resort to this if they have problems? This is literally banned in a few countries! I would feel more guilty than before by drinking this. It gave me such bad chills!

"Do you have any more?" Ester asked.

"Yeah, I have some here. You want it?"

"Why would I be asking if I didn't want it?" She aggressively gave another bottle to Ester. She chugged it easily. While she wasn't paying attention, I spilled the rest on the ground. Good riddance. She shouldn't have this. Why did she spend one thousand dollars on this? Wait, isn't vodka super cheap? How high-end is this vodka?

Vanessa put the rest in her bag and pointed her thumb at me and Ester. It signaled that we had to leave. I skipped along with them, curious about where we would go next.

Yeah, we went back to school.

We arrived fashionably late, and all of us had different classes. Coincidentally, my next class was with Drew. I want to show him the recording today. It would be to my convenience so that this problem could end as soon as possible. If we can do this today, it would remove one of the main problems. It would be much easier to stop her if Drew is out of the way. That way, she won't have to call her knight in shining armor to save her. What can she do if she doesn't have a knight in the first place?

It was science, with the worst teacher ever, Mr.

Damien. You know that I hate every teacher, but this guy is beyond that. He will remove points because you talked to a student in class weeks ago. How messed up is that? He uses the same excuse: *the past affects the present.* His classroom looks weird as well! He has science gadgets all over the place. They're not the cool ones, like a real-life periodic table. He has at least eight lava lamps sitting on one shelf. That is enough explanation. We have assigned seats in his classroom. He puts the wise students in the back and the slackers in the front. Yours truly is in the back. And unexpectedly, Drew is in the back. He isn't a jock or bully anymore, more like a nerd.

Scratch that.

He's a jock that cares about his education. That's very, very weird.

That's very, very abnormal.

The classroom has green everywhere, which makes sense. The stereotypical color of science is green. These glazed orange and brown cabinets have transparent glass to show what's inside. One of them is dedicated to the cursed lava lamps. The classroom has no rug, which makes it impossible to rock your chair without getting hurt. One of the most annoying parts of this classroom is the chairs. It involves the odious ones that are always picking on your hair. I've lost so much hair to these chairs. One desk in the corner has Mr. Damien's desk for working. It is messy, with papers all over the place. One stack of papers unironically has a mug on top. The mug says "world's best teacher," which is a lie. Ugh, why is it all lowercase!? It should be "World's Best Teacher." The font is bubbly and colored red. There are individual rows of desks, evenly spaced out. The classroom is so hot that I always keep my water bottle. Imagine going to this class after history. The front of the room has a mega whiteboard with a small magnetic basket full of markers. Black, green, red, and blue colors sat inside the basket. The left side of the board was full of notes from his last lecture, which he quickly erased with the classic black whiteboard eraser. He had a spray that removed any traces of letters. Each desk had a vandalized wood top. There was slang on the desk. The farther back you go, the less slang. (The nerdy kids don't like to vandalize.) The classroom doesn't have warm linen lighting. It has a bright, pestering white light. It makes it hard to fall asleep.

 I had no idea he had a brain in the first place with his absurd decisions. We don't sit next to each other, with Sheldon bordering us. He often harasses him with what he did to Connor. Nobody popular except him is in this class. This is my chance to show him. When Mr.

Damien finished his lecture about the properties of matter, he gave us an assignment. I knew I could partner up with Drew, and while we were doing the assignment, I could show him the recording. There was an empty desk next to him, so I sat there.

"Hey, Drew! Would you like to do the assignment together, just the two of us?"

"Uh, uh, ye-yeah. Sure." Drew doesn't commonly stutter with his speech, so this confused me.

"Question one: 'How is a chemical change different from a physical change?'" I waited for him to answer.

"Physical changes are those where the shape, size, or state of matter changes. Chemical changes are where one or more substances are combined to make a new substance."

"That's the perfect definition!"

We continued until we finished. Drew is lazy, so instead of asking for a new assignment, he sat in his seat and used his phone.

This is perfect. Now I'm closer to Drew. Now he truly trusts me.

✧ Chapter Twelve ✧

When I entered school, all eyes were on me. Again. Drew gave me resentful looks, and Vanessa talked to Ester. I started to advance to Vanessa, wanting to speak to her. I waved at her, but when I was one step away from her, she left.

"H-hi, Vanessa!"

"Hey, how's life going?"

"Good."

"Got a good taste of that vodka?" She questioned.

"Ugh, really?" I scoffed.

"Haha," she laughed.

I walked away from them, and when they couldn't

see me, I had Violet approach me. I nudged her to come.

"Is the plan going well?"

"Spectacular." We went silent for a few moments.

"Well? Spill the tea already!"

"Okay, so first, Vanessa and Ester are starting to get the hang of me. Sure, they keep making fun of me and joking about my strong dislike of alcohol, but it is coming together!"

"Great. The school year may end soon. We have to finish this." Oh yeah, that's true. It's almost the end of May, and the school year ends in June. I've been delaying this for too long. Oh, why haven't I been keeping track of time? I'm such an amateur.

The bell rang, so we had to leave for class. I waved goodbye to Violet, walking away.

All my classes were bland except for history, where something *interesting* happened. Mrs. Trapini had her usual lecture and gave us an assignment when she finished her lesson. She was handing out the papers when she said this.

"Mrs. Trapini! Monica and I have to go to the bathroom. Could we be excused?" Vanessa appealed.

"Be quick!" She replied.

Vanessa grabbed my wrist and dragged me out of the classroom. We went into the girl's bathroom. I guess she trusts me enough to go to the bathroom with me.

"I'm having an end-of-year party this weekend." She handed me a pretty pink invitation. It had a bow on top. The invitation listed her address and said "End of Year Party!" The font was serif, and it was a dark aesthetic pink with glitter all over it. There was a rose border. This theme by Vanessa is getting overused. Yeah, it is what makes her shine, but at what cost? At least five other students have this same theme. The only reason she stands out is because she can take this theme far. She should switch it up to be blue or something. What a cliché.

"We will sit in the popular student lounge together. Are you accepting it? Or are you a loser?"

"No, no, we can sit together." I hesitated.

She stomped outside, and I let a deep breath out.

Wait a minute...

This is my chance. I *can* embarrass her—a fatal blow at her own party! Anything that happens here will be remembered forever, buried in the depths of Willow Creek history. Every student would remember the path I chose. I could be considered a legend. You know what? I know *exactly* what to do. This will either be the worst decision I ever make or the best.

✧ ✧ ✧

Mom jumped when I told her I would go to a party. After all, my past self would never go to one. But remember, this is the new Monica. I left to change my clothes. I knew I had to wear the most unique outfit I could find. Something that would make me jump out of the crowd. Well, then I remembered that I couldn't pick my outfit yet. I have to do my skincare first. I picked up my cream and smothered it on my new smooth, creamy face. I may have snuck into Mom's closet and put on some makeup. Only a bit! I put on a bit of blush and used her black eyebrow pencil. I used logic to put them on, even though I don't know how to wear makeup. I put on my favorite light pink lip gloss. I looked in the mirror and saw my face popping out of a crowd, showing *true* beauty. I winked at myself in the mirror and left her bedroom. I skipped to my festive closet. I stared at it long and hard until I figured out what to wear. And let me say, this might be one of my favorite outfits.

 I chose a sparkly white dress. Its iridescence would make me the star of the show. I wore these white shorts. I did a little dance in the dress. It was so cute! I was comfortable with my clothing appearance, but my hair was a cluttered, tangled wreckage. I got my most expensive hair straightener and turned it on. I let it heat for a few minutes and planned where to straighten.

When it was sizzling, I went to use it. I first straightened the bottom parts of my hair and went through the rest. I did burn my ear a bit, but it will be okay. Beauty is pain, and it will disappear in a moment.

When I looked at the finished product, I liked it, but I felt it was missing something, and a lightbulb appeared above my head. I needed to wear jewelry! I went to my jewelry box and looked for the most over-the-top jewelry. I chose these long earrings that went down to my shoulders. It comprised three dangly rows, each with gems on it. It was like those earrings celebrities wear. I wore a necklace that Mom got for me a long time ago. It had a golden chain, and this charm was in the middle. The charm was a transparent glass square with an eagle in the middle. It gave me nostalgia, but I couldn't recall why. I wore, like, six or seven bracelets. Each of them is custom, with my name on all of them. I felt ready when I put on this beautiful headband. It had gems on it and roses. For my shoes, I wore diamond heels with precious rainbow stones reflecting on the front.

I was ready for the party. It struck 6:00, which was time for me to leave. I shouted Mom's name, and she came down. She said I looked good. We went outside to drive there. When we entered the car, I ensured I had everything I needed. My phone was in my pocket. I thought about the party and how Vanessa wouldn't expect what I would do. It is the exquisite element of surprise.

You may be wondering about my plan, correct? What is it? You're a lucky person. I'll tell you about it. I want to *embarrass* Vanessa and those stupid popular kids. I will put them in their place, where they deserve. Since I am popular now, I can easily manipulate myself into their shoes. This will make my job so much easier. The first part of the plan is to become, you guessed it, Vanessa. You know that recording I took of her? I'm showing it to Drew. How will she get her savior to help her? Besides, dating someone like Drew gives her 50% of her popularity. Now, Vanessa will obviously have a deejay there. I have asked people about the best parties; they always have deejays. You need one if you want a memorable party. So, I plan to be a witch and knock out the deejay. Tell me, how else could I get the microphone? Then I will roast the heck out of Vanessa, Ester, and maybe Drew. You know what? Why can't I forget about Chad and Bradley? Who knows? Perhaps I will help Connor with his situation. Violet, as well. Oh, I almost forgot. I have to ruin a few *extra* lives as well.

Do you like my plan?

When we arrived, there were these two

bodyguards outside the door. It had stanchions beside the steps. I could hear the booming of loud music at the party. The bodyguards had these stylish black glasses that people in spy movies wear. They wore a black suit and tie, feeling classy. They didn't wear any hats. I went up the steps, hearing my heels click and clack. They had their hands behind their back, curling them.

"You here for the party?" His voice was loud and clear.

"Yes, I am!"

"What's your name?"

"Monica."

He spent a minute finding my name on his list.

"Here you are! Have a good time!" Don't those rich people from the movies have a list for a party? He opened the door, and I was met with a red carpet. I entered the home with sparkles all around me. My eyes were blinded. Disco balls were hanging from a thin silver chain connected to the ceiling. There were the staircases around me. The hallway led to an area that looked like a club. It had a disco floor, with multiple colors flashing randomly. There was a bar on the side, with shelves full of alcohol. The full bottles of liquid were concerning. Numerous people were sitting on the bar stools. The dance floor was full of people. I had my eyes wide open, gazing at the area. The front of the area had a deejay playing music, and he had a microphone in his hand, which was ethical for my plan. I saw Vanessa, Ester, and Drew all out in a lounge that was unique for them. Connor was there as well. There was a "V" on each side of the mixer. On the side was a foosball table and a few booths for people to sit in. One said, "POPULAR STUDENTS ONLY!"

I have to embarrass them close to the end of the party. That way, everyone will remember it. I can't be too early. I could ask Violet if my decision would be moral. I know Violet will be here. She loves parties. I went to look for her. Violet told me that she comes pretty early to parties. I found her sitting at the bar bench, holding a bottle of alcohol.

"What the hell are you doing? Did you forget that drinking is illegal?" I shook my head.

"Who cares? It's only one time. When will I have another time to try it?"

I crossed my arms.

"You idiot. Anyway, forget about your drinking. I have a plan."

"What is it now?" She whined.

I told her about my plan, and she looked pleasantly surprised.

"That ... that might work. You should try it." I was about to speak, but she continued. "If you use your plan, however, there will be one thing. Don't you even dare involve me in this!"

"Okay," I winked at her. She rolled her eyes and went back to drinking.

"Oh, wait! I almost forgot." I handed the necklace to Violet.

"How did you get this?"

"I have my ways."

I left her, wanting to have my own fun. I went up to Vanessa, Drew, and Ester. They were sitting in their "popular student" lounge. We were at the first part of my plan: to get Vanessa to lose Drew. Oh, I am going to hate this. I will never forget this event, that's for sure.

"How's it going, Vanessa?"

"Good. Come, sit. You're so weirdly formal."

"Shut up!" She shouted. It was so loud that nobody heard her. Hundreds of students were screaming, having the time of their lives.

I sat next to Drew, thinking about my life, when I saw Violet. She was signaling me to show him the recording. I pulled it up on my phone, ready to strike.

"Drew, I have something to show you."

"Yeah? What is it?"

I played the recording out loud on my phone.

"Vanessa? Is that true?"

Vanessa was boiling.

"What the hell are you doing!?" She screamed, but nobody heard her. "You aren't supposed to do something like that! He got me so many bags!"

"Wait, what!? We are so over," Drew shouted. Everyone was watching. I was a little panicked, so I walked away quickly. Oh, but it didn't end there.

She started to chase me.

She pounced on me like a cat, trying to punch me. This is only the first part of my plan, and it's already this messy! She pushed me to the middle of the dance floor, where we were seen fighting. Her face was hilarious! Her angry face looks so weird! I punched her in the face a few times. She ended up ruining my hair and wrinkling my dress. She punched and kicked me a few times, but nothing too shabby. I ended up with a few scars, but whatever.

It was shocking how weak she was. Everybody was cheering for me. It felt amazing to have this attention! At the end of the fight, she ended up bruised. A few scars were on her cheek, and a big red spot was on her forehead.

After the fight, I brushed off anything on my arms

and went to get some water. A battle with the most popular girl in school can get you thirsty! I went to the water station and poured myself a cup. Suddenly, Violet came around me and patted me on the back.

"That. Was. Epic."

"Hah, thanks."

I stayed with Violet. We were having a fun talk, and we chilled. I invited Connor to sit with us. We sat in the club's corner so nobody would notice us.

"Hey, Connor!"

"Monica ... you look stunning."

"Hah, thank you."

I cracked a smile. We talked for an hour, but it was time for my big announcement. The deejay was asking for song recommendations, where it would be perfect to strike. I could effortlessly lay a punch on him without anyone noticing. I took a deep breath, getting ready for what I would do.

I went up to the mixer and stood next to the deejay.

"Hey, deejay! What's your name?"

"It's Henry. You got a song?"

"Yeah. It's called 'I'm about to punch you.'"

"Wha-" I hit him, brutally bruising him on his face. That left a big red mark.

I looked for the microphone. I found it and grabbed

the handle. It was all black, with the handle shining. Standing there made me feel on top of the world. I was shining like the sun, having all of the attention. I took in the moment and decided to start my fun.

"Uhh, is this thing on? Can you hear me?"

"We can hear you!" Someone yelled.

"Alright. So, you guys know me, right? I'm Monica." Violet was watching me, shaking her head.

"What's going on?" Vanessa yelled.

I have to be quick!

"So, I got a few words to say for you."

"Spill them already!" Someone was desperate to hear what I was going to say.

"First of all, I will call out a list of names. Vanessa, Ester, Drew, Chad, Bradley, Alexandra, Eloise, and Chantelle. Every person I listed is one type of person: a dumb witch."

Everyone gasped at my comment. Violet gave me a thumbs up, Connor was confused, and most importantly, Vanessa and Ester were flaming.

"Those two girls you keep idolizing as the coolest students in school? Well, they have some juicy secrets!"

"Uhh, what do you mean?" Vanessa trembled.

"I have some tea to spill about her. Vanessa dates a new person every week because she wants money! She spent 1,000 dollars alone on alcohol, including vodka. Ester is using Vanessa for her money, and, oh, the cherry on top is that Vanessa asked me to help her with history! She's about to fail the year. Let me tell you, I'm not even scratching the surface regarding her deeds."

"W-what!?" Everyone stared at Vanessa, and Vanessa looked at Ester.

"Do you want to know the actual cool students? The ones who aren't as driven from power?"

"Yes!" Everyone shouted.

"Well, Connor, Violet, and Colette are all on my list. But you might be wondering: why Connor? Didn't he bully all the students? Well, let him answer that." This wasn't planned, but it would define all of my respect for him. I called Connor up to the stage, and he joined me.

"I have changed. It is because of this beautiful student who helped me define my ways. Be honest; raise your hand if you dislike Vanessa."

Every student raised their hand proudly like a flag.

"This girl helped me change. We need to idolize students like her in our school. I have stopped all of my bullying, and I will prove it. I even got a taste of it! We can't keep supporting people like Drew or Chad. These students caused all of our drama. Justice for Monica!"

They assume that everyone likes them. In reality, we all resent them.

Connor started to chant "Justice for Monica." Violet joined him and walked up to the stage. I stood in the proud middle while they were on the sides. Soon, everyone chanted my name, and it felt oddly soothing. Everyone started to resent the popular students.

I was a nerd and became popular.

Vanessa lost everything.

Do you know what this means?

Mission accomplished.

"Revenge is the act of passion.

Vengeance is an act of justice."

-Samuel Johnson

About Ferwa Muhammad!

✧ ✧ ✧

I'm a twelve-year-old girl who wrote this whole book. My dream is to be a young writer. Well, it came true! Determined to get this on sale, I made this my top priority. After hours of writing and hundreds of skipped recesses, I finished the manuscript. Instead of leaving it as it is, however, I went and finished the other parts! I edited it and designed the cover myself.

I wrote this for one reason: to tell everyone that nobody can tell you what you can do. Don't let the status quo influence you. Don't let yourself down. You can get through everything you're going through. I would recommend you start writing. It is fun, and it can be very relaxing. It helped me feel better after bad days.

Oh yeah, shoutout to Abigail (Abby) Domenica! She read my book and told me what needed editing.

Shoutout to Emily Avakian as well! She's the coolest :)

To my grandfather: I'm sorry that I made Monica's grandfather dead! I still love you with all my heart!

To my dad: I'm sorry I didn't include you! I don't know why. Don't worry, you're still the best dad ever!!

To my mom: you're amazing and the nicest person ever! I love you!!

Oh my god. I can't believe I forgot to thank you for reading this! Sorry for my late thanks. I am thankful that you chose to read this esteemed piece of writing. This piece cost me six months and my blood, sweat, and tears. Thank you for taking the time to read this. From the bottom of my heart.

With a delightful tone,
Ferwa Muhammad

PS: There is more work coming soon!

Stay tuned... ;)

Made in the USA
Middletown, DE
05 June 2024